The Man Who Lost His Gayness
and other stories

David M Hancock

Abysmal Antics Publishing
NEW YORK

www.AbysmalAntics.com

Cover art by Vila Design

"Far Away, And In Someone Else's Ass" was published under a different title in POZ Magazine, 2005.

ISBN-13: 978-0986437519
ISBN-10: 0986437514

Library of Congress control number: 2015903665

From "The Prodigal Prince":

"My son."

The queen, his mother, swept into the receiving room in a rustle of black and gold finery. With a well-practiced flourish, she held out her knuckles for him to kneel and kiss in the courtly manner. Still fuming over his rough summons to court, he did not. After a moment she took back her hand and turned away from him until the serving ladies retired.

"Your manners have grown coarse in these years away. It is ill-done to shame a queen before her servants."

She looked tired. And older than he remembered. Though still beautiful, there was a looseness to her skin he'd never seen before. Shocking tributaries of silver threatened to swamp her auburn luster. That was her pride, he knew, of all her charms – her crown of thick red hair.

She in turn was regarding him: His stringy flaxen mane, longer than the fashion; and the blue eyes, his father's eyes, cornflower blue. Thin, flat-chested and altogether too small for his years. He could see her critiquing him as the product of her body; noting how the last five years had changed him. And judging how best to bend him to her will.

Tired, yes. And thin. But still churning with the irrepressible energy of her ambitions.

What was she up to, this warrior in women's robes? What was she plotting, this schemer? Was it as Jonathan said? Was he to be married off to some minor princess?

I am not a boy anymore, he told himself. I am a grown man of 25 years. I will marry or not as I choose, queen be damned! Only I must be careful, for she is full of guile and manipulations.

Also by David M Hancock:

Novel: Tricks Gone Bad

Coming:

Poems: 50 At The Orgy

Novel: The Downcast Prophet

The Man Who Lost His Gayness

I Don't Know Why

The guy is taking too long in the bathroom. Extra time to regroup might be warranted if you had butt-fucked. But this had been a quick suck and swallow. Dude: Do a gargle, take a leak and bounce. Don't spend 20 minutes doing your hair. And don't burgle the medicine cabinet.

And you? How are you feeling, now that your little guys have delivered their load to market? You old dog, you. Having any of that retro shame over committing an intimate act with a stranger? Or are you still in your 'Life is beautiful, grab all you can get' mode that has served you through the middle ages. Yes? Feeling the joy? Good call. Kudos to you, pal. You're an old fart with a big dick and you just got off with a twentysomething.

How would you rate it: This latest of the many anonymous BJs you have enjoyed in your life. You'd give it a "B," right? Of course, you only give As and Bs. Every blow job is excellent or meets expectations. There are no lower marks.

He was a little strange, though; and a little rough. A bit of the tortured, self-loathing flavor about him. He hadn't been pleased when you opened the door. No one is; those days are over, honey. But he was willing to do the deed, in a nihilistic 'Everything is screwed up including this' way. Within 30 seconds he was on his knees, and it was all over in five minutes.

Isn't technology wonderful? People who want to hook up ASAP are using GPS apps to find other people in heat near them. Tiny signals bouncing off satellites; the modern equivalent of a bird's raucous call or the pungent aroma of a rutty baboon's swollen red ass. Little faces on your phone, an online catalog where the merchandise – except for a few time wasters – is ready to move. Same-day delivery.

Here's the door opening, finally. Your young trick comes out. He's Spanish looking, or Italian. He's got a lot of product in his hair giving it bulk and waves. It was crunchy in your hands. A Sal Mineo type, the doomed gay loving James Dean in "Rebel Without A Cause."

For the first time, you notice he doesn't look well. He's extremely thin and his face is pallid and shiny; clammy with the sweat you get when you're nauseated or having diarrhea.

"I was just washing my mouth out," he says. "There was a lot of blood in my saliva."

Pause.

"I don't know why I keep doing this," he says mournfully, looking down.

Uh oh. Here you were patting yourself on the back for successfully closing another deal. Starting to think about a little din din. And now a perfect afternoon just got complicated.

He looks at you, waiting for your reaction. Is there something he wants here? Does he want to be berated? What the F is going on?

Well, if he wants to be crushed under your heel, he's picked the wrong fella. You take 100 percent personal responsibility for any risks in this arena. Freaks, crooks and all.

During the blow job he had looked up at you in the submissive manner made popular in porn by both male and female cocksuckers. Wide-eyed, questioning; how am I doing, daddy? I love it.

In retrospect, knowing what you now know, his presentation had been a little hostile. Joyless black eyes looking up at you.

You stare at this young man, wondering if he purposely tried to infect you with HIV. With his rough, toothy technique, and his bloody saliva. Is he acting out against whoever gave it to him?

More likely he's just a pitiful sex addict who can't put on the brakes even when he's sick. Not like you, a centered, self-realized Dionysian with impeccable scruples.

Or is this malicious twat just trying to freak you out? To get even with you for being old and disappointing. A manifestation of that post-coital reflex of unevolved young gays. Reject the act that just occurred, and spurn the person you did it with.

He does look ill, there's no getting around that. Why would you put your precious penis in a diseased mouth?

Whoa there, steady fella. Remember what you were told by your doctor, that jolly queen who specializes in AIDS and HIV. Could you get HIV from receiving a blow job, you'd asked. Not unless they nick ya, he'd said merrily.

And you've had your dick sucked by dozens and dozens of poz partners. Some of the best, most worshipful drainings have been rendered to you by cocksuckers who were doubtlessly positive. If that was dangerous, you would have gotten it long ago.

What to say to this trickster? What do you say to someone who is sick?

Do you need anything, you ask. Imodium, or a glass of water?

He shakes his head. Is he disappointed that you're not wigging out? He collects his jacket and

3

shoulder bag. He's quite a fashionable twink for a serial killer.

After he leaves, you go to the bathroom and wash yourself in the sink. Crack out the rubbing alcohol. You inspect your penis for abrasions and find none.

Not feeling so grandiose anymore, are you? This is what they mean by safer sex; as opposed to absolutely, 100 percent, goddam guaranteed safe sex.

But I wouldn't let it worry you, chum. If there was blood in his saliva, then there has probably been blood in other cocksuckers' saliva. It's not the greatest thing in the world to have positive blood rolling around the skin of your dick. But it's not like it was covered in blood – like Carrie at the prom – when you took it out of his mouth.

And doesn't saliva deactivate HIV? Haven't you read that?

You'll be fine. Three months from now you'll get a test and put this behind you.

And if it does go against you, if the dice finally come up snake eyes, you'll deal with it. This is not 1982, God damn it. You'll have plenty of treatment options. You'll stay on top of it from the very beginning, every step of the way.

Of course it would be humiliating to stumble this late in the game, after all these years of artful dodging. Not you, oh great and powerful Oz.

And you wouldn't have the privilege anymore of typing 'I'm neg' as part of your sales pitch.

I don't know why I keep doing this.

What should you have said to him? What should you have said?

The Man Who Lost His Gayness

Judy, bless her, got it wrong. There are lots of things sadder than the man that got away.

For instance, take this dismal queen: The man that won't go away.

For a half-hour I've watched, while sipping this annoyingly watery martini, as he launches himself here and there in this bar; like a bumptious sheep dog scattering the geese.

Here he is again, drink in hand, trying to ingratiate himself with that trio of startled twinks. As if. Look at them, making phony-nice chitchat, their faces pursed as if they were passing three particularly dry turds.

Even he can feel the ice when they turn their backs to resume their conversation.

You gave it the old college try, chum. But you, in your decrepitude, are profoundly out of your depth. There's a reason they call this place Barracuda; the cuts are razor sharp. Beauty rules and everyone else gets schooled in this crowded, dim corridor of a bar in fabulous Chelsea, New York City. Home to more poofs, posers, preeners and pretenders per square-inch than most anywhere in the world.

Uh oh, here he comes.

Rough night, he says, pulling a stool up next to me at the bar. He orders a vodka cran like the vampire he is.

Can I buy a lady a drink?

I smile vaguely without making eye contact and shake my head.

When it arrives, he raises his glass to me.

Here's to scaring all the gaybies, he says ruefully. Beware the Ghosts of Christmas Future.

I nod and clink his glass. I can't bear to be rude. But it's depressing that he's including me in his circle of failure. If I keep it dialed down to a minimum I might still escape this encounter.

But he will have his chat.

How about you, he says. You look very hot in your ... what is this look, Sterile Cuckoo?

Thanks, I say. It's more Junie Moon. Without the scars.

That subtlety is lost on him.

Having any luck?

I'm waiting for a girlfriend, I lie. I'm just looking at the scenery.

He snorts derisively. For the first time I see a crack in his forced good cheer.

In my day, I wouldn't have looked twice at any of them.

Since there's no escaping him, I take stock of my new acquaintance. I try to imagine what he sees when he refers to "my day." He has his hair, I'll give him that; a crew-cut thatch of sandy-brown fading into white. That's about it, the rest is forgettable: a broad forehead, a squat nose about 10 years shy of bulbous; big horse teeth and sun-tanned skin (with the age spots that go with it). He probably claims 35 on the hookup sites he doubtlessly trolls back home in Texas or Florida. But I would put him north of 45. He's a salesman, I bet. The kind of guy who pressures you to buy because you feel sorry for him.

Maybe, if I'm being generous, I might cast a younger him as an extra in a sailor musical. Some dancing gob in the background, making love to a mop. There is nothin' like a dame.

You want to hear a story, he says. Let me buy you a drink – he gestures to the bartender at my martini – I'll tell you something strange that happened to a friend of mine. See what you think.

As a Republican candidate for governor in my home state of Texas once famously said: When rape is inevitable, just lie back and enjoy it.

My friend, he says, was just an ordinary gay guy. He'd gotten past the trap of marrying a woman to hide. He had dodged the epidemic. He could handle his alcohol; and not much taste for drugs. Just an average Joe who liked to be on top of things. He didn't have a boyfriend but he was satisfied with his life. He was doing okay. And then it happened.

What, I ask, as I raise my new martini.

And my persistent acquaintance undertakes to tell the tale that I present here, with embellishments.

Looking back, Laurence could precisely pinpoint the place and hour he first realized he'd lost his gayness.

It was a Sunday afternoon, Feb. 27, in the Fort Lauderdale apartment of a man with whom Laurence had been corresponding on the Internet. Negotiations had proceeded satisfactorily to the point where Laurence was attempting to insert his half-hard penis into the man's lubricated anus. For some reason, the usually reliable Laurence found himself wilting within his wrapper. In desperation he'd sought a mental totem to stem the ebbing tide and shore up his faltering erection.

He saw a pussy.

On Feb. 27 in a Fort Lauderdale condo,

Laurence envisioned a pink, wet pussy fringed in damp brown curls. An engorged cunt with two plump labia and a seed-pearl clit glistening in the frothy stew. In his mind's eye, his face instinctively drew nearer to sniff and lick the musky rose.

His dick stiffened.

Thus buoyed, Laurence had finished matters with the Fort Lauderdale man. But his vision had left him troubled.

Why are you telling me this story, I ask. Is it a joke? Is there a punch line?

Oh yeah, he says ruefully, there's a punch line.

Laurence thought this strange disorientation might pass, like a summer storm of the psyche; blows in hard and then evaporates. Maybe it was some oedipal thing working its way through his system, now that his mother was gone. Her death the year before had freed him of the last throes of guilt at disappointing her. Was this some twisted last-ditch attempt to please her? Had her death highlighted his own mortality to the point that he was resurrecting long faded hopes of being a father?

It seemed plausible in a subterranean, Jungian way. But it wasn't enough to explain the complete swing in his libido, the potency of his desires.

His desire to perform cunnilingus was particularly troubling. Like many young gays, he'd stuck his face down there a time or two to salvage a floundering encounter. His memories of all that had blurred into a mélange of youthful panic and cunt smell.

Not like now, when his heart beat faster at the thought of lapping the labia. Stick his nose in and tongue out and root around down there like a pig digging for truffles. It made him hard thinking about it. As a gay it was beyond comprehending; as a straight it was as natural as saying grace before the meal.

He kept catching himself in hetero moments. At the porn shop, his feet would wander to the big jugs section. He got it now. When he was still trying to pass, he used to pantomime his joyous face diving into the cleavage of a bodacious rack. Make the noise of a sputtering motorboat, bluh, bluh, bluh, as his cheeks were slapped back and forth by imaginary knockers.

But that had been theater for the straights. Now he imagined how it might feel: The tactile thrill of big boobs.

So many things he understood now. The trashy porno blonds and Asian chicks making goo goo eyes as they sucked dick. He used to think they looked ridiculous. He got it now: The freedom of impersonal behavior with a woman. Yes Daddy, I'm your nasty bitch and I'll do any sick thing you want.

He bought titty porn and whacked off frantically. He watched jugs video on his computer and spilt copious loads onto the wooden floor below his desk. The porn dicks were nice; their presence was required. But he just didn't feel a connection beyond seeing them as part of the fauna in the landscape.

The desire to eat pussy, more than anything, drove Larry to seek out a live experience, to test this confusing new impulse. Maybe it was like when he started eating ass. Something that had seemed so disgusting ten years ago had become enticing. Maybe eating pussy was part of a late-stage progression to pansexuality? Was nirvana just ahead?

He thought about trying to pick up girls in bars; but he didn't feel he had the moves or a plausible backstory. He envisioned going to a titty bar; but that would just cost a lot of money. And probably end in a powerful jack-off session at home afterwards.

He turned to the Internet, familiar ground to find new prey. He cast his nets upon the seas, looking through both high- and low-brow sex sites.

As he plotted how to turn fantasy into a real event, Laurence hit the first hitch in his transformation to straight guy. As a heterosexual neophyte, he tumbled head first into the whore-madonna pit. He could think any number of salacious thoughts about a woman's body in the abstract. But any real woman he might actually meet who so shamelessly enjoyed sex in all its wonderful manifestations was a dirty used-up slut.

As he looked at the faces and tits and pussies on the Web, he imagined his face coming up scabrous and peeling after diving into some diseased honeypot.

Vaginas were incremental repositories of contamination; while men shed the consequences of each encounter.

You friend didn't just turn straight, I say. He turned sixteen. That's some pretty basic wrong thinking.

You'll see, said the storyteller.

He knew it was unfair. It manifested the most primitive societal mores against women. A woman taking ownership of her sexual power; it should make him hot, not make his dick shrivel. He would never apply that bondage to any of the men he had tricked with; or himself.

He wanted the act. He wanted a woman. But he didn't want an experienced woman who would compare him unfavorably with her other lovers. But he didn't want a novice. It was confounding.

He finally settled on a "Jenny" who had an earth mother quality about her ad. He found her on a site that professed to offer healing sexual work but let anyone sign up and advertise. Jenny was a hooker but seemed sweet. In her picture she had a lean, tawny body with bunny breasts. Hooters, it seemed, were best left to the tawdry imagination.

Here it is, he thought fearfully, as he opened his apartment door to Jenny. Touched for the very first time.

Jenny was as good as her pictures. Maybe women were more honest about that on the web, who knew? Her brown hair was cut short, which gave her a slight butchness. Her arms were sinewy but soft; as they undressed he saw she had a quarter-inch growth in her arm pits. He didn't know what he thought of that; but it wasn't an automatic turnoff as he would have said in his gay days.

When they were naked, he drew his hands lightly upon her body, raking her skin with his fingernails. He circled her breasts, his fingers tracing a spiral path up to the two berries. She gasped as he pinched them and he got his first whiff of her arousal. He cupped her small breasts and buried his face in them. Bluh, bluh, bluh.

She insisted on using a condom to suck him, which was disappointing. He could feel her mouth on him, pulsating and squeezing; but there was none of the delicious liquidity to slide things along. In the same spirit of overkill, he put on a surgical glove from a box he kept for the cleaning lady and fondled her. He wasn't quite ready to go muff-diving; he had noticed a small wart on one of the labia. And she was, after all, a real, bona fide whore; not a normal woman wronged by his ignorant prejudice.

He sat back on his heels on his bed as she curled her naked body around his thigh and delivered her faux blow job, his hand between her legs.

While she was awkwardly mouthing his wrapped meat, Larry found himself thinking about the many great blow jobs he'd had from devoted cocksuckers. Guys who would park his dick at the back of their throat, pulsing their tongue and mouth on his shaft and squeezing the cockhead with the trachea opening. Men who knew how to worship dick. No condom for them; they wanted your cream, insisted upon it.

Laurence's deflowering was occurring in the bedroom of his second-floor condo, which had a small Juliet balcony overlooking a parking lot and a canal. Moonlight coming through the sliding glass door was shining on the white wall above his headboard, casting a silver frame around a peacock feather pinned at a 30-degree angle. The beam of moonlight would quickly travel out of his room; but while it was here, the feather seemed to glow. There was a faint sparkle here and there, as if a tiny lightning bug or two were nestled in the black and green tendrils.

Laurence had gotten the feather a few

months ago during a one-day cruise from Port of Fort Lauderdale to Utopia, a new tourism island created by the government of the Bahamas. The online ads had featured a huge water slide at one of the new hotels, and lots of shiny people smiling as they sipped vividly-colored cocktails.

He'd bought two tickets, hoping that impossibly young thing would come along. But their tenuous connection had faltered before bon voyage time. The wasted $99 had cast a pall on the outing, as he threaded through the casinos and bars of the cruise ship "The Discovery." There wasn't a gay onboard except for a few femmy waiters. Even the weather was off, cloudy and ominous.

They docked at an amazingly long pier that extended far enough to sea to allow the big ship to pull up and disgorge her throng of families and scornful teens and snow birds.

From the pier they were herded past bars and curio shops and fruit juice stands towards a generic street market; a charmless concrete plaza with dozens of tented stands arranged in a grid. It looked like a flea market from Anywhere, U.S.A. Laurence wandered mindlessly with the pack, taking in the placemats woven from palm fronds, coconut shell carvings and brightly-colored clothing.

He was on the fringe of the field of tents when the squall blew in. He had been looking at a sparse offering of feather jewelry and ornaments. The proprietress was an unsmiling black woman with gray hair. Her offerings were roughly made and crude: a leather cord knotted into a necklace featuring a black raven's feather and some beads; wall hangings featuring feathers and sticks which might be Caribbean dreamcatchers.

She seemed to specialize in feathers. He had commented on one of her pieces, a white circle woven of sea gull feathers and sea shells. She had answered him unsmilingly in the sonorous creole of Haiti, quoting him an exorbitant price. She was one of the blackest people he had ever seen; the whites of her eyes and her teeth seemed to glow by contrast.

He had to jump fast to grab the end of her tent when the wind got it. He held tight as the wind pulled hard, billowing the canvas into a parachute that threatened to lift him off the ground. As the rain started, the old woman scrambled to put away her wares while he kept them dry for her.

She had given him that feather pinned on his wall. The battered peacock feather with its indigo eye lined in electric aquamarine. The deep blue eye that was watching even now as he changed his position to ease the pins and needles in his legs.

Unsmiling, with an angry look on her face as if she hated being obliged to a white man, the street fair woman had waved the peacock feather three times over his soggy head. And then his landing party was being rushed in the rain to the hotel where they would have an authentic island buffet before making an early return to Florida.

The rectangle of moonlight had moved down the wall, illuminating the lovers tableau on the bed. Jenny gasped as he thrust his four gloved fingers hard inside her, thumbing her clit as if it were a door buzzer. The sound of her cries drove him into a frenzy. Within seconds he was bucking on top of her with no thought of trying to last. Amid the chaos he took note of how easily his cock slid inside her, how well everything fit. With his eyes still on the feather,

14

he convulsed uncontrollably and squirted his virgin load into the rubber.

In that moment of resolution, he saw it.

The Haitian woman in the Bahamas had done it. She had waved the feather, chanted and taken his gayness.

But was this cleansing a gift or a curse?

Oh, is this a parable, I ask. I thought this was a real story.

It is a real story, he says. Hey guy? Another round?

After the prostitute, Laurence decided to go aboveground with his lust. He was a man after all. A single man with working equipment. How hard would it be? Wasn't it a single man's world? Weren't there ten desperate women for every eligible straight man? He was just playing it wrong, like the loner he was.

He put the word out to a couple of his women friends: Anna, the wife of his second cousin, and Laura, a trusted former co-worker. He was "post-gay." He was over it. He was looking for an understanding woman who wanted a connection. No fag hags. He wanted companionship that would include sex, he had to keep reminding his matchmakers.

When he was younger he'd had occasional "work wives" – women he'd bonded with, safe in the understanding that nothing romantic could develop. It would be like one of those deep, confiding friendships – but with the added possibility of landing in the sack.

Or so he imagined.

But there weren't many takers for a longtime

gay man who had suddenly had a change of heart. At least not among the pool queried by his two co-conspirators. The women doubted his sincerity, his friends told him over tea. These women of a certain age – he'd told his friends not to go too young, he didn't want that – didn't have the time to help him work out his issues.

They don't believe it's something you can change, Anna had told him, using her "tell mama what's really going on" expression that he found so annoying.

Some women couldn't deal with the HIV, AIDS connection inexorably tied to gays. After being set up on a date, Laurence spent a long evening discussing hypothetical safe sex with a woman, only to have her shiver with rejection at the idea of sleeping with a gay man. He had tried to explain that she should be having safe sex with every man. That she should consider, as he did, that every partner was positive; and take action accordingly. And then not worry about it.

Another woman was fixated over herpes. She didn't believe him when he said he had never been tested. He thought about saying he supposed he had it but it wasn't a big deal. But that obviously would not be a comfort.

No sale, he'd told Laura in the post-date analysis.

It's a fine line how much to go into on a first date, Laura said. It takes time.

In truth, herpes was still a bit of a bugaboo for him, too, in his ongoing quest to eat pussy. With men you could scout the terrain pretty easily. Women were all tucked away. They didn't reveal themselves until you were knee-deep in the mud.

He decided to take matters into his own hands and approach women in bars. Perhaps their screening techniques were more abbreviated and of the moment then these set-ups his friends had been giving him.

But he found, rather, that many women in bars had bullshit detectors dialed up to maximum. If a man was hot, he imagined, they might go ahead and fuck him as a one-off. But an ordinary looking guy had to jump through hurdles.

Saying he was single and just hadn't met the right one yet didn't fly for someone his age. Invariably the conversations would keep circling back to inquiries into his past. Had he been married, why wasn't he married? Had he any long term relationships?

Something about his story would invariably sound fishy to them, and he would see the light of interest die in their eyes.

So much chatting. So much talking. He found it exhausting. Such a tedious way to be rejected, like a cat playing with a mouse. So different from men, who were more visually oriented and quicker to let you know how things stood.

He thought about fabricating a plausible back story. Married for eight years, no kids, divorced for seven ... Had played the field but now looking to settle down ... Looking for a nice woman who wanted kids.

What was it they said in sales? Fake it til you make it.

But he was determined to be truthful in this new chapter. That was the one thing he prided himself on in his gay life: He wasn't a deceiver. He had never tricked a woman into being his beard.

Laurence didn't know what he was in the hetero world, and it showed. He also wondered if the wildness of being gay had ruined him for straight life.

He met Wendy while waiting at the Wholefoods checkout line. Three separate lines of shopping carts had inched their way to the finish line, waiting like race horses in the starting gate to be summoned to a free cashier.

Just as it was Laurence's turn to go, a middle-aged Asian woman clutching a loaded shopping basket darted out of nowhere to his intended cashier.

He exchanged amused glimpses with a chubby man on his left, and a girl on his right.

"Hey, Ching Chong, we're waiting in line over here," whispered the girl, just loud enough for Larry to hear. She was a hippy girl, broad in the beam, with muscular thighs and fat arms. Her large bosom jutted impressively perpendicular to her chest. A single girl, about 35, with brown curly hair and a sarcastic gleam in her eye.

"Oh, me no understand," he whispered back.

At a coffee date, they continued their bashing of the Chinese.

He told her about something he's seen one time driving into New York City, via the Holland tunnel from New Jersey. He'd been in the next lane over while an Asian man, with the straight hair and stark features of a Mongol, was pretending to not understand the EZ Pass system for collecting tolls. The man's face was contorted in fear like a great thespian, portraying obliviousness to the need for a little white device on his windshield that would signal the toll gate computers to bill a linked credit card account. The Asian man held the aces in that he was perfectly willing to hold up traffic with his feigned ignorance. Laurence knew he was pretending; and so did the tired cashier who finally waved him through.

On the other side of the toll booths, the man's face had burst open with mocking delight at beating the stupid American honor system once again.

Yeah, said Wendy, so primitive. Makes his day to save 25 cents.

She told her story, about the two Asian girls that would always leave her yoga class early to beat the crunch of people putting away their mats. Even though the instructor asked each time that people not disturb the final repose by leaving early.

She asks them not to do it, and they just look at her like she's not there.

What about the country, said Laurence. All they do is steal. Intellectual property rights? Forget about it!

Well I'm glad they had a cute meet, I say. But I'm starting to fade here.

The bar is thinning out. It's a Thursday night getting long in the tooth. The stars have lost their glitter. If mama is going to find a husband, she needs to get cracking.

There is something unstoppable about this one, though. A Midwest forthrightness to speak his piece. Hmm. I wonder how big his is.

Please, he says, I'm almost there. I promise. Bartender?

So, in the fellow racist, Laurence found a girl midway between sinner and saint. Wendy was a freelance graphic artist who lived with a talkative black-and-white tuxedo cat named Cicero. She also moonlighted as a tax consultant. She offered to do his taxes, which got them off to an unusually honest start.

You're just as poor as I am, she'd said with a good-natured snort of derision.

Wendy had a single tattoo, on her left shoulder blade: A realistic, if vividly cartoonish, depiction of an exit wound on her freckled brown skin. The back side of a bullet through the heart. He found the inked carnage, the ripped muscle, torn skin and spatters of blood, oddly dramatic for such a low-key girl.

Wendy was unique among the small pool of women he'd met in that she didn't require a backstory. They had made a deal early on not to drag out their past partners; but he had never expected it to stick.

But Wendy was notable for her low expectations. He could call her or not call her, cancel at the last minute, or fail to help with promised favors of auto expertise or manly lifting powers. It didn't faze her.

Like a new tenant feeding the neighborhood feral cat, she gained trust by expecting nothing. No sudden moves, no attempts to grab.

He came to see that for many women, having any man was better than none. And a single woman in her 30s with saddlebag thighs and slightly sagging breasts couldn't be too choosy.

Maybe that was the secret behind her wound tattoo. When he asked about it, she just shrugged, closing her eyes and pretending to pick something random from a sketch book.

But maybe what she didn't want to say was

that she'd had some kind of searing epiphany. She'd lost the sweepstakes. There would be no husband and children for her. And as a single woman, that made her second best to any woman who had a man. Perhaps the tattoo was expressing her internalized shame and self-abasement as an unchosen woman.

It was like the starting point of most gay children when they realize they are different from the other kids. A feeling of inferiority; a sense of brokenness, incompleteness.

The realization of his possible worth in Wendy's eyes, little though she might let on, made Laurence feel powerful and valuable. It lessened the regard he showed her. It was a diminishment that, paradoxically, freed him to be sexier with Wendy. He could act as he pleased with her, since she didn't matter. She could be his launching pad to hotter women.

He took a deep breath and submerged his face into her, joining the great society of cunnilingus.

When she got pregnant, he married her with a near delight at the quaintness of it; the old-fashioned abnegation of personal choice. It was like he was floating in air, watching events unfurl for the person in his body. He was just an ordinary Joe, after all.

This is too much. Is he about to crack out the family photos, I wonder. My tuck is starting to pull loose; but there's no way to adjust it without a lot of deconstruction.

He can see I'm getting impatient. I signal no with my hand over the glass when he tries to get another martini started.

21

Flash forward 15 years and Larry's in the backroom of a gay bar, trying to get some unseen cocksucker to service him.

And it's not because he's been secretly gay all along and his mind was playing games. He was gay first and he was satisfied. Then he changed to straight and learned to live that way. He still likes pussy, you know? It's just ... he got bored with the sameness of it. The same person all the time. And no wildness, he missed that. Meeting someone and having sex right away. The ease of it, the spontaneity. It was so easy with gay men.

And there it was. It hit him. The punch line.

The one thing he had prided himself on, back when he was gay, was that he had never tricked a woman. Never been a closet case misleading a woman, refusing to sleep with her and making her believe it was her fault. Pretending to be straight and then sneaking around.

Except there he was in the dark room, seeking some connection she can't give, as he prowls among the kneeling figures, looking for a welcoming mouth.

My relentless friend's story sputters to a stop. He looks at me to make some ruling on what I've heard. There are so many layers of confusion and deception it's hard to zero in. I reach for his left hand to shake it and his face falls.

But I'm not leaving yet. I just want to check something. Yes, there it is on his sun-tanned ring finger, the pale white shadow of a life he's set aside for tonight.

I understand what he's trying to say. Forget

about all the peacocks in this bar, parading about and pecking each other. There's so much more to being gay than posing or sucking dick. It's a lifestyle, a mindset, a sensibility that can't be reset just because he's changed teams.

Being gay is the kinship of outsiders. Membership in a secret fraternity where the walls of race and money and culture come down under the common bond of shared lust. The fierceness of those not bound by conventional relations. The adventure of growing up with a secret. The camaraderie of knowing what it's like to be on the outside of society; and letting that empathy inform your actions with compassion.

It's tribal; sitting in a hot tub with a hard prick in each hand and two on yours. Looking up at the stars and feeling effervescently alive as swirling sexual energy roils the air jet bubbles.

To be gay is to live like an artist, even if you're not. A world where a creative man can wait tables during the day; and in his downtime scribble poems and stories that will never be published. And then tape his penis flat and be celebrated for parading about as a woman. A profusion of lifestyle choices, liberation from proscribed behaviors that don't fit or feel good.

Being gay is having a private life devoted to lust. The danger of opening your door to a stranger. A world where you can electronically send a picture of your dick to a stranger and expect to see his on reply. Dancing in a strange city at 2 a.m. amid shirtless men with wandering hands. The thrill of finagling a threesome; and the disaster of being excluded by the other two. A world where a mediocre one-night stand can become a superlative

23

friendship for life. The unknowability that infuses each new encounter.

Think of it. Twinks turning into trolls that still score occasionally with twinks. Just as they had occasionally let some troll get lucky back when they were twinks.

The great circle of tricking renewing itself.

This man has lost his gayness. I will give him mine.

I will share my pie with him. He can thrust his hands in and gather the berries and crust into his sticky mouth. I know what it is to hunger for it, as he does tonight, in his limited window of opportunity.

As his fairy godmother I will grant his wish tonight. Come to the cabaret, old chum.

I will suck his dick in this bathroom while making slutty goo goo eyes. If it's a nice one, I will lead him home and let him fuck me with his straight cock. Or more likely, he may want his chance to get fucked. No matter. He can pretend that this man dressed as a woman is his wife wearing a strap-on. How about that?

I will rock his world in the spirit of gay men everywhere, servicing each other's lust with a smile. I will send him back over the rainbow, renewed and refreshed, to wifey and kids and his black-and-white life.

All this and more, so help me! Or my name is not Liza Judy Gale!

One thing, I ask.

What's that, he says.

What about the feather?

It's away somewhere, packed up. My wife wanted to throw it away but I wouldn't let her.

Have you thought about burning it?

Why?

Might break the spell.

Something for him to think about as he gets his rocks off tonight.

I grab the Ghost of Christmas Future's hand and lead him deeper into the bowels of Barracuda, towards the ladies' room with the lockable door.

Jinetero: A Cuban Romance

Donny refrained from jerking off for four weeks before the trip. He didn't know why, it just seemed the thing to do. By flight day he was a jangle of pent-up sexual energy. His body felt juiced with testosterone and his thoughts were tinted in trippy orange hues of horniness. He felt a little high, marijuana buzzy high, and filled with a sense of magical potential over his first visit to Cuba.

Not that Havana needed any of his sexual energy to be a magical place. She did fine all by herself at being both sexy and magical. Her fame was legendary worldwide – a city frozen in amber from the 1960s when Cuba's economy went off the tracks into a parallel dimension of government-run enterprise and Soviet Union subsidies. Donkey carts and '58 Thunderbirds, crumbling Spanish architecture and ration books; Havana moved at her own antiquated pace, an enchanted kingdom living under a spell of ideological poverty amidst the hustle and bustle of the Caribbean.

I say she. Havana is a woman, don't you think? Havana is an African woman, *una negra,* with firm breasts and gleaming white teeth. She parades down the *Paseo de Marti* with a twitch in her hips, music in her legs. She slits chicken throats with her knife and sings praise to *Oshun*, goddess of love and gold. Havana is the *Malecón*, the ocean boulevard where Cubans throng each night to take the sea breeze. On the *Malecón*, Havana struts with an invitation in her eyes; and, if you're not watchful, a cock up under her skirt.

26

Apart from its mythical status as a surviving Communist regime, Cuba had an extra sheen of perception for Donny. His interactions with his Cuban American co-workers in South Florida had polished a new facet on the Cuban diamond, a rancor towards Fidel Castro that expressed itself in a desire to strangle Cuba economically. As the song goes, we all hurt the one we love. And nothing was truer of that than the twisted love-hate relationship between Cuban exiles in South Florida and their Castro-controlled motherland.

As an Anglo American transplant from California, Donny was not deeply invested in the gnarled politics of South Florida's Cuban exile community. He wasn't well-schooled in Latin American governments but suspected a lot of them were privileged empires which did little to raise the quality of life for their poorest people. It had been his impression that the Castro regime had made advances in health and education for its people, despite the unworkability of its communist economic model.

But he quickly learned to keep such thoughts to himself. There were powerful forces in the exile community that dictated a hardline approach against Cuba to Washington, the Florida media and academia: Castro's Cuba was an abomination that must be crushed.

In 1991, the year in which this story takes place, there was a lockdown on trade between the U.S. and Cuba; no immigration policy other than that if any Cubans made it alive to Florida shores they could stay; few travel visas in either direction; and strict limits on the amount of aid exiles could send to the island. Telephone service was spotty, mail was slow and a flotilla of exiles was waiting to sail into Cuba the day Fidel Castro died. Rescue their relatives, reclaim their homesteads; it was all a gauzy exile dream that Cuba could go back to how it was.

Cuba was pummeled under a double whammy in 1991. Not only was she denied the lifeblood of her northern neighbor, so close but so aloof. Longtime comrade the Soviet Union was imploding and had dramatically scaled back its aid to the island. Cuba's glamour as a soviet outpost on U.S. shores had faded over the decades since the Cuban missile crisis. Yeah, it was fun to piss off the Americans by being so close. But the soon-to-be dissolved Soviet Union wasn't going to actually do anything against the U.S. – other than import a little Communism to the region.

But all this diplomatic bullshit is only marginally in Donny's brain as he boards the plane for the 55-minute flight from Miami to Havana. After all the hype and mystique and second-hand smoke, he's finally going to see it for himself. Cuba, you lovely island, island of tropical breezes.

Around him on the plane are his colleagues from the Dade County community college where he teaches Spanish. Enforcers of the exile hardline, first-generation Cuban Americans balancing their disapproval of the regime with the excitement of seeing the homeland of their parents.

At the Havana airport there are soldiers in green army fatigues and combat boots with machine guns slung over their shoulders. The government officials are brisk and unsmiling. On the shuttle bus to the hotel, Donny takes mental notes from his window – the old cars, the cracked cement highway, the occasional potholes. The wooden peddler carts,

donkeys and horses here and there. The buildings –
a mix of square-block Socialism and charming
Spanish architecture – need paint desperately.
Havana has good bones, but she needs some
primping.

They check in at their shabby hotel, and then
it's on to the academic conference they are attending
– one of the few wiggle holes for American visitors in
the U.S. fence around Cuba.

We can skip through the details of the
conference, an earnest symposium that has served
its purpose in transporting Donny past the sentries
on either side of the Straits of Florida.

Let's move forward to the end of Donny's
second day in Havana, where he is strolling down the
Avenida de los Presidentes towards his hotel of the
same name. The boulevard has a strip of grass in the
median, nestled with statues and gazebos and sitting
areas, stretching from the waterfront to downtown
Havana.

It's a sweaty late afternoon in May, overwarm
from an absent breeze. All along the avenue are
beautiful, if decrepit, examples of Spanish
architecture – pastel and white palaces with
balustrades and minarets, colonial relics that Donny
will soon discover have been occupied by squatters
and subdivided into smaller apartments.

Walking ahead of Donny is the title character
of this story, a young Cuban man in his mid-twenties.
He looks back at Donny and smiles. He looks back
again and waits, and the two are soon talking as
they stroll towards the sea front.

Our young Cuban is named Juan Carlos. He is
very handsome. He has crisp wavy brown hair that
sits high on his head, green eyes and brilliant white

teeth. Like many of the Cubans Donny has observed, Juan Carlos is wiry and lean. And a little hairy – a thick clump of brown hair peers from above the top button of his *guayabera*, and his brown arms are a jungle.

Juan Carlos asks Donny if he would like to *conocer*, to know, his apartment. Donny's heart leaps with excitement. Wasn't this what he was looking for, walking along the avenue? And now it's happening so easily!

Juan leads him to a large two-story white stucco building. As they enter, a woman across the street yells something to Juan, who angrily answers back. At Donny's raised eyebrow, Juan explains that she is the head of the local *Comité de Defensa Popular*, a committee that monitors the actions of its neighbors.

She has scolded me for bringing a tourist to my apartment, Juan says with the frankness that Donny will quickly grow to appreciate.

She can see you are not one of us, he says, gesturing at Donny and his blondness. I sent her to the devil.

The apartment must have once been some kind of museum or social parlor; the front door opens to a cavernous room 40 feet high that has now been divided into several two-story apartments built from plywood and two-by-fours. They take stairs on the right up to the one main room of the apartment, a bright, large space bounded by a plywood floor and ceiling. There is a table with three chairs and a few other chairs in a sitting area. At the center of the tableau rumbles an ancient refrigerator.

Two of the three large windows are bifurcated by a sleeping loft held up with strategically placed four-by-four posts. The placement is such that the light is divided between two levels.

In the room is a man who is obviously Juan Carlos' father. Same wiry build, hairy chest and arms. They shake hands and make small talk. At one point Juan walks over to the refrigerator and opens it, showing a glass water pitcher and little else.

You see, we have nothing to offer you, he says with a smile.

Juan tells him that his parents are divorced. His mother is in poor health and lives in another part of town. His father has lost his job; Donny can't quite catch what the profession was. There was a sister who left in the Mariel boatlift in 1980 when she was 16, and communication is only sporadic with her.

Juan invites Donny to see a performance of the Cuban National ballet that night. As an American, Donny cannot go by himself; but Juan can get the tickets, he says. After only a moment's hesitation, Donny says yes.

Donny shakes hands with the father, and Juan leads him down the stairs. Juan stops midway on the steps and regards Donny with a quizzical look. As he passes him, Donny plants a quick kiss on Juan's lips and continues down.

From that kiss it is on, as the young people today like to say about something fast-igniting and exciting.

The ballet, which costs the American equivalent of 25 cents a ticket, is superb. The theater is three-quarters filled with Cuban men and women dressed to the nines, as well as very modestly dressed folk. It's a happening scene; a real cross section of the population. Donny feels like he's stumbled through some glamourous door into Cuban

31

high society, a different kind of elite that isn't only about money.

As they sit in the audience – the handsome blond American and the Cuban escort – Donny imagines secret service agents taking note of his identify. Checking to see if this *gringo* is blackmail-worthy. Or is he being too paranoid from all the propaganda he's inhaled in South Florida about Cuba's police state. But what about Juan's description of the c*omités*, the KGB-style block chiefs spying on their neighbors?

The thought crosses his mind that this is a dangerous game. A presumably wealthy American making the scene with a tour boy. A *jinetero*. Donny is no fool, he knows which end is up. He's heard of them. *Jinetero*, from the Spanish for *jinete,* horseman. Your new friend in Cuba to help you with all your needs.

None of it seems to matter. He's in Havana having an adventure. And sex is in the air.

After the ballet, Juan walks Donny back to *El Presidente*. Donny is of a mind to bring Juan up to his room and ravage him. But as Juan had told him was likely, there are armed guards beside the elevator and stairwell. The prostitution police.

They part chastely. The next few days are a whirlwind of sin-free outings, a virtuous courtship spent at museums and walking along the *Malecón*. There's never a place or a moment to be alone. The fever grows between them.

As the elder of the two – Donny has a tendency to be a little stuffy, a predilection that will only get worse with time – Donny makes it his mission to put some meat on the young Cuban's bones. Which is easier said than done because the food in Havana is awful. The ingredients are suspect. Donny has had more than one meal where the meat component was vague, perhaps even inorganic. Juan tells him there is a rumor going round that pizza vendors are cutting up condoms – which are in easy supply from the clinics – and putting them on the pies to crisp up like cheese.

They are having lunch at one of the tourist restaurants – there's a separate tier of hotels, stores and restaurants where Cubans can't go unaccompanied – when Donny asks about AIDS and safe sex.

Juan has just finished describing his friendship with an older man in Mexico City who visits him occasionally and sends packages of clothing, food and household supplies. It seems to Donny that Juan is explaining a workable model, should Donny be so inclined.

Juan is very up front in explaining his life to Donny. He operates under the principle that he is *jodido*, screwed, and has to make the best of things.

Aren't you afraid of AIDS, Donny asks, using the Spanish acronym SIDA. It's 1991, and every gay is afraid of AIDS.

But Juan Carlos is nonchalant. He says he gets tested regularly at the clinics. Donny asks about *Los Cocos*, the controversial sanitarium where Cubans with AIDS or HIV are forcibly sent.

Juan shrugs and Donny can see that to him it is just one more thing completely out of his control.

In the hotel lobby one night, Donny runs into a colleague who chides him over his absences from the conference.

Maria is Donny's academic "buddy" for the

three years he needs to get tenure at the community college. She is just a teacher herself, but that hasn't stopped her from wielding her power over Donny. It is Maria who has seen the liberal chinks in Donny and firmly set him straight.

There you are, Maria says to him, as he is returning from an afternoon spent with Juan. Where have you been, she asks, with just a touch of the school monitor in her voice.

Donny debates what to say and then, easiest of all, speaks the truth. Or at least part of the truth, which is a wonderfully subtle way of lying.

At the National Museum in Old Havana, he says.

This is such an obviously superior choice over an academic panel, that it shuts Maria up other than a "see you tomorrow."

On Saturday night, Juan takes him to a discotheque on the other side of the *Malecón* from his hotel. As he gets out of the cab, Donny is greeted by several teen-age girls vying for his favors. It's yet another establishment where the Cubans can't go in without a tourist on their arm.

*Jinetera*s, says Juan gayly.

More than a few. More than two dozen, mostly girls, and so young. It makes Donny a little queasy to see these tricked-up teenagers on the make. And a few men, sexy boys who stare at him, all waiting outside the club for a tourist to take them inside.

In the club, they have a rum and coke. Donny comments on the scene outside. Juan laughs and says he is different from those *jineteras*.

Lo que no entra aquí, he says, pointing at his eyes, *no entra aquí,* he adds, pointing at his mouth.

They are there early and the club is half empty. Donny finds it a little depressing and primitive, all black paint and flashing lights and mirrors. When he goes to the men's room, he finds an L-shaped urinal lined with a back mirror from foot to waist-high. He would be able to see every dick taking a piss in this intimidating mirror; but fortunately there is just one man on the far side of the L. The man, a type of Cuban wolf so prevalent in Havana, watches in the mirror intently as Donny manages to piss. Is he a cop waiting for Donny to give one too many shakes to his wang? Or a hustler Donny could add to the mix for $20? Who can say.

Juan is proud of the discotheque in the manner of a third-world person who thinks his American visitor can only appreciate the newest technology. Donny conceals that he finds it dismal, and manages to move the evening in the direction of a walk home on the *Malecón.*

It is their final night together. They walk a little way and then sit on a shallow rock wall, looking across the ocean, north to America. Waves gently batter the rocks below the sea wall; a little way down, some black Cuban kids are jumping off rocks into the surf. The breeze is cool on their faces. Behind them blares the noise of the boulevard, the cars honking and pedestrians arguing.

I could throw myself in the sea, says Juan dramatically, *me tiro en el mar.*

It is the era when Cuban rafters by the thousands, *balseros*, set out in inner tubes roped together; hoping to survive the sharks and sun and reach Florida shores.

But I could never leave my mother, says Juan.

Of course not, he says. It's too risky, anyway.

Juan begins to cry discreetly, and Donny pats his shoulder, watching fearfully about for police.

They get up and drift along the shorefront. Cubans are drinking and smoking weed, and a few men are giving Donny the eye – as if he would dump Juan right there and upgrade models. There are some real flamers, too, raving queens who don't seem afraid of the bored police who pass by here and there.

With unspoken accord, they turn off the *Malecón* and walk down one of the streets leading to Juan and the father's apartment. Donny spots a darkened hallway of an apartment building. They enter and find a corner out of sight from the street and begin kissing passionately. Donny thrusts his tongue into Juan's mouth and the boy sucks on it hungrily. Donny returns the favor. Their bodies press against each other urgently, this way and that, until there is not one glimmer of space between. At the sound of a door knob turning, they break from their clench and rush back to the street.

When they reach Juan's apartment his father is still up, smoking a cigarette. Donny shakes hands with him, and then the father retires to the sleeping loft above. The light from upstairs soon goes off.

Juan motions Donny to sit in the "nice" chair, a comfortable straw recliner where the father had been smoking. Juan brings him a glass of water which he drinks from and then places on a little table next to the chair. The father's tobacco is in the air, a sweet smell different from the acrid cigarette smoke of the U.S.

He watches as Juan kneels between his legs and begins unbuttoning his pants. No words are spoken as Juan slides Donny's pants down to his ankles, followed by his white boxer shorts. Donny is already half hard when Juan takes his prick into his mouth, with a soft murmur of approval at its size.

It doesn't take long before Donny is squirming in his chair, his hands clenching and unclenching to signal to Juan his impending release. With a shake of his head, a gesture beloved to men everywhere, Juan shows his intention to stay parked on Donny's dick and take the load in his mouth.

Remember that this tale is set in 1991, an era where there was much more suspicion of oral sex than today. In their talks, Juan had been so well-informed on safe sex practices that Donny is a little disappointed at this imminent lapse.

But since Donny knows his own status as negative, he decides, with seconds to spare, to let loose now and lecture Juan later.

With a quiet whimper, he convulses and squirts four prodigious blasts of cum – one for each week of abstinence – into Juan's mouth. He watches with satisfaction as Juan's eyes widen and cheeks bulge from the unending onslaught of semen.

That's how we do it in America, boy, he says silently, with a little of his mother's Texas twang thrown in.

This little story could end right now and it would be the tale of Donny's most memorable blow job. And that would be a very beautiful story to tell, don't you think? An adventure in an exotic land, an emotional connection with a handsome new friend, a hint of danger and reprisals – it's all sauce for the flame.

Donny watches limply as Juan Carlos staggers over to the sink and spits out a heavy-sounding gob.

Que rico, Juan murmurs, as he rinses his mouth. Like many Cubans, Juan can roll with the punches.

In a daze, Donny pulls his pants back up and finishes his water. They make plans to meet Sunday for lunch. It will be their final date; Donny's group flies out at 5 p.m.

Back at the *Presidente,* Donny is opening the door of his room when he hears his name called. Looking down the hallway he sees Maria, his community college colleague, gesturing for him to come over.

Where were you, she asks.

The group from Dade County had been scheduled for a final dinner at *El Morro*, the Spanish fort overlooking Havana harbor. Part of the notorious prison has been converted to a fancy restaurant. Even without Juan on his mind, it had seemed odd that so many anti-Castro exile children would bend their scruples to dine at a place where enemies of the regime had once been jailed and tortured. Or maybe even still, while they ate their black beans and plantains.

Not my thing, he says.

I brought you something. Come, says Maria, grabbing his hand and pulling him into her room. She seems a little drunk.

She presents him with a small slice of chocolate cake wrapped in a napkin. Maria is dressed in a red-and-black halter dress. Her full breasts are unfettered beneath the cloth, and she wears a yellow hibiscus bloom tucked behind one ear amid her flowing black hair. Maria is embracing her *Cubanidad,* he can see, with her sandals and flower and loose tits and hair.

Look, she says, pointing out her window, isn't it beautiful?

They lean out her window and look at the full moon over downtown Havana. Below is the *Avenida de Presidentes* leading towards the downtown lights. He can see statues here and there, glowing pale white like ghosts. A breeze cools his sweaty brow and traffic noise and music floats up from below.

You've been brave, running around the city by yourself, she says, twirling a strand of her hair on her finger.

Chocolate and sex. It occurs to Donny he isn't the only one to invest sexual energy into Havana.

With a thanks for the cake, he beats a hasty retreat; leaving Maria to join the long list of disappointed females taken in by his ambiguous sexuality.

After the magnificence of the blow job, it is almost to be expected when the true consummation of their tryst is anticlimactic. Isn't that the way of the world sometimes? A man wins the object of desire and then loses interest?

When he arrives at Juan's apartment the father is not there, for a change. What must it be like to have to leave your own home so your son can turn tricks with tourists, he thinks, surprised at his cynicism. It is as if all the magic of being in Havana has drained out of him along with ... well, you get it.

Juan leads him upstairs to the loft, a low-ceiling space where the tops of the windows from below provide a strange ground-level light. Juan cautions him not to stain the sheets on the bed where he will later sleep side by side with his father.

As he gently fucks the Cuban boy, Donny tries to imagine the two of them living together in his tiny studio in Miami Beach. Donny working at the college, Juan studying English. Teaching Juan to drive, buying him some beat-up wheels. Juan getting a job as a waiter in Little Havana or some other area where his lack of English wouldn't matter.

The domestic scene grows more ghastly and stultifying as he reviews it. Both of them quickly getting bored with each other and conducting affairs on the side. There are other considerations, too, although Donny is not honest enough with himself to acknowledge them. After unwrapping his gift, Donny has been a little put off by the amount of wiry, coarse hair covering the boy's body and ass. He is a real little werewolf. Even with the condom, working his cock inside had been like penetrating a briar bush. And Juan's cock is less than optimal, narrow and curving up.

No, it wouldn't do. If Juan had been a complete Adonis, largely endowed with wispy body hair, would it have been different? Would Donny have taken a stab at a doomed long-distance romance, writing letters and sending care packages?

Hard to say. They part tearfully with promises to write. Donny presses some American dollars into Juan's hand, although truth to tell, he has little left to spare.

A few hours later the Dade delegation is shuttling through airport security. They are almost to their plane when a customs inspector spots the cardboard three-pack of Cuban rum that Donny has bought at the duty-free store. The official, a sour-faced rogue, confiscates the bottles and takes them into a room while Donny waits. A minute later he returns the box to Donny with a scowl.

It isn't until that night, back in Miami Beach,

40

when Donny opens the cardboard carrier and sees a healthy slug of rum missing from one of the opened bottles.

It's that story, har har, that Donny will tell his friends when asked about his trip to Havana.

Yes, he tells the filched-rum story. And the crappy food and the condom-pizza story, and the potholes and long lines of people waiting for rations. He even gives a modified version of the KGB neighborhood spy committees. These all fit in with the company line about corrupt and repressive Cuba.

Donny never tells anyone about the young Cuban he befriended, the *jinetero* who accompanied him on his explorations of Havana. The trip to the ballet, the night club, the walks through Old Havana and on the *Malecón*. Ice cream at *Coppélia*. A son supporting his ailing mother and unemployed father, doing what he can with what he has. The beautiful young man who cried tears over their parting, and with whom Donny fell in love with, just a little.

All that stays unspoken along with Donny's many other secrets.

Donny never answers any of the half-dozen letters from Juan, one of which includes a traced cutout of Juan's shoe size. They are beautifully written in cursive penmanship, reminding him of the emotional connection they had shared and detailing the commodities most lacking in Havana.

This little story could also end here, with the dismal guttering out of the tiny spark between the Cuban and American boys. Except for one thing: Maria. Remember her, the strident *anti-Castrista*, who let down her hair and defenses for Donny on a moonlit night?

Maria takes affront at her dismissal. In the

way of people of a rigid nature, her attraction turns to antipathy. Maria makes it her business to spread stories at the college about Donny's hijinks with a *jinetero*. She must have seen them together, walking here or there near the hotel, and put it together. Or heard something from one of her operatives.

Putería y mariconadas, is how she puts it, whoredom and faggotry.

Without a single slip of paperwork, Donny is blacklisted from the college. When the spring semester ends, he waits fruitlessly for his summer school assignment. In August, he is told his contract won't be renewed due to budget cuts.

This is a lie. There are the same number of Spanish instructors as ever; he just isn't among them.

Thus begins a long and draining period of economic uncertainty in Donny's life. The teaching job had been a crappy one, all in all. But it was something, and carried a small amount of stature as one of the noble professions.

What follows are a succession of jobs Donny is ill-suited for in temperament and ability. As well as several humiliating economic rescues by his parents, who provide aid but also soul-sapping remonstrations.

But no curse lasts forever. In America, if you keep trying, something usually comes your way. Donny eventually drifts into PR and marketing, where his glibness and Spanish ability find purchase.

As the years pass, he seldom thinks of Juan Carlos, in the way people are reluctant to do after they've turned their back on a friend or relative in need.

When he does think of Juan, he wonders if

the Cuban has managed to wade towards kinder shores, as Donny has after his difficult years.

Or is Juan still trapped in amber, living in a frozen economy as the U.S. stranglehold on the island endures through Bush 1, Clinton, Bush 2 and now Obama. As he walks amid the crumbling mansions and potholes, how is Juan faring as his handsome face fades? Is he still lean, or has he grown bloated and corpulent like the narra- ... uh, Donny?

One thing Donny can never quite decide is how thoroughly he'd been played by Juan. He knows that if he ever told this story he might be scorned for a gullible fool. Emotional manipulation is part of a good prostitute's tool kit, after all. And there had been a slight practiced quality to Juan's tears on the *Malecón* that night. Surely he had gone on to the next tourist soon after Donny left, probably had a stable of friends sending him aid. Donny hoped so, anyway.

However sordid they might seem to an outsider, Donny's memories of Juan and Havana retain – even after all these years – a very innocent quality to him. Particularly looking across a vista of too many Internet hookups with creepy cyphers

It was a friendship, above all else.

In a way, Juan represents the best qualities that Donny has come to appreciate in his Cuban American friends. Frankness, earthiness, toughness.

Survivors.

So ends the tale of Donny's best blow job ever and Juan Carlos the Havana *jinetero.*

The Unnatural Sister

Magic is coming into our world. Its arrival is not fixed like the train at 10 and 2:15. Nor stark, as a new baby ushers in irrevocable change. Uncanniness is swirling about us as a wave pushes violence and froth upon the shore. Magic, occasional and aloof, in your backyard like a stray cat with many benefactors but no master.

Some say it is the stars. A new era has dawned, bringing a gradual infusion of chaos into the fading age of modernity. Others feel the shift more abruptly, as if a powerful spell has been newly set upon our time. Or a dusty curse broken at last.

No one knows how or why. We share only an unspoken unease that something strange and fierce is incontrovertibly taking hold.

Most of us pretend nothing is happening. Indeed, there seems to be a glamour upon the change, a compulsion not to think or speak of it.

The TVspeaks tried to keep up with the changes, at first. There were reasons, they explained brightly on our retinal feeds, that people burst into flames. Neurochemical imbalance caused by exposure to pesticides; secret tests of a North Korean death ray.

It could be scientifically rationalized when people turned green and reptilian; or hairy and sharp-nailed. A Chinese RNA virus, a Russian toxin. A jihad.

The faders were harder to explain away; the faders and the statues. That took the starch out of the TVSpeaks, forced to narrate the surveillance camera views of this or that person fading out of sight. And the home videos uploaded by families of someone who had ceased moving and gone stone-like.

The TVSpeaks grew sullen recounting the increasingly inexplicable events of the day. The roundup of faders, statues and screaming human bonfires. Lots of other strange shit. I know you know what I mean.

For some who try to make sense of the madness, a Solomonic logic reveals itself. It is as if people are more clearly expressing their truest selves - sometimes with disastrous consequences.

Events, too, are more emblematic of their inherent nature. Walls and rivers appear between quarreling communities. Conflicts of war are epic. The dramatic arts are thriving and acts of kindness – or malice – are rewarded threefold. Actions have consequences; it's hard to just coast along anymore.

I'm telling you these things, dear reader, so you will accept my story. That I recognized the sister at first glance. Her mystical nature, all that she was – and wasn't.

If you're to follow this tale, you must press on past any reluctance to acknowledge magic. Magic is in every corner of this story. Please focus. Open your mind.

The sister of the woman I hope to marry uses the human name Elena. When I began courting Beth, I believed her to be the only child of a wealthy retired publisher. I am some years older than Beth. A chance flirtation we enjoyed many years ago now serves as a bridge in her eyes to the man I have become. A link that sets me apart from the other fortune hunters lurking about, now that she is in her

30s and must make a decision about children.

I mention her father's wealth freely. It is a consideration. I find Beth charming and I can see a happy life for us, built on the bedrock of her father's money. Every marriage is a bargain, a melding of different assets to a single cause. I bring her my spark, my seed; she gives me a home, a shelter from the coming storm.

In this, as in every age, those who fare best are the ones who can adapt. People like me, who come from nothing. I could tell you my name, but more informative would be that I come from nothing. When you come from nothing, anything is gravy. For a nimble man, a light man, this time of change brings opportunities with the risk.

Although Beth has not yet accepted me, our understanding has progressed to playful discussions of what our futures might be like, entwined. I bring up kids a lot, to keep her eye on the ball. Money, I tell her, is only a tool and must not be used to judge someone disparagingly. The presence of money creates possibilities for bold choices.

It is in discussions of the future that one can gauge a person's awareness of the turbulent present.

Like many of this time, Beth can consciously accept that our reality is changing. She remarks on it, this or that queer event, but retreats mentally from the larger implications. I see her as one in the vanguard of those struggling to awaken. It's a tricky matter, like a chick breaking its shell. Best to let it arrive in its own time and effort.

My first sign of the trouble to come occurred a few weeks ago. After holding off as long as I could, I had begun taking Beth to my place, a glaring symbol of the gulf between us. I have a small, functional burrow in the downtown. My morning view is a parade of pedestrians' feet carrying their owners to their daily affairs. On some days, an odor of urine rises from the concrete steps descending to my basement.

I can't pretend there is no disparity in our circumstances. I can only minimize its weight; keep reminding her my poverty is only one of many ingredients in the mix.

We were on my sofa with my cat, to whom Beth was surprisingly indifferent, sharing a retinal feed of the weekly Jill Slinger Cataclysm Report.

Jill is one of the last TVSpeaks trying to make sense of the dawn of magic. She tries, bless her heart, to cover the unexplainable as a linear news story.

Her diligence has taken its toll. Smart, polished, authoritative; Jill was once at the top of the news heap. Now her unwillingness to move onto pleasanter topics has relegated her to semi-crank status on the RealityView retinal news feed.

Jill's latest angle was a quantum physics scenario that included overlapping dimensions bulging into our own. Like loaves of bread baking side by side, the crusts merging.

But her heart wasn't in it. She had a scattered air about her, and a grim look as she opened the show. As Jill unveiled her hypothesis, her eyes kept darting to something off screen. As the camera pulled back, a small winged creature could be seen flitting over her desk. When it landed, we saw a tiny figure on two legs waving its arms at Jill. It almost seemed to be taunting her – until Jill's fist came down and crushed it.

"Wake up people!" screamed Jill as they cut

to commercial.

"Well!" said Beth. I waited for more but there was none forthcoming.

When the show came back, Jill was gone. They played a canned video stream of the day's news. We watched a feed about a "Modern-day Moses" who saved dozens of lives by redirecting a flash flood with his walking stick. Then followed a report of a police crackdown on a nest of reptilians. Homegrown terrorists plotting an attack on the harbor. The narrator cued up the perp walk, and out they came, each one more lizard-like than the last.

At that, Beth jumped from the sofa. I followed her into the kitchen, where she was shaking as she ran hot water in the sink.

"They don't know anything," she said, furiously scrubbing a plate. "They act like they do, but they don't know anything."

It was soon after that she told me about her sister, and we made plans for a meeting.

On a late fall afternoon I set out for the first time to her father's house. The concrete sidewalks and asphalt streets of my downtown lair give way to cobblestones and dirt alleyways as I climb a hill overlooking the bay. My city, which I had thought to be San Francisco, becomes more what I imagine London to be. A Charles Dickens landscape of horse-drawn carriages, gas street lamps and evening fog.

The sister is installed in a family brownstone in the old money part of town. The building is u-shaped; two windowed parlor rooms protrude out to the sidewalk on either side of a broad stoop where two stone greyhounds look down upon the street.

Do they own all three floors? Even as I thrill

at the stench of antique prosperity, I wonder what I will find in the newly revealed sister.

After passing inspection by the silent dogs, an elderly footman takes my overcoat. Beth leads me through the landing into a receiving room of gleaming oak floors and an expansive ceiling. Several doors lead to rooms away from the hall; a large polished staircase curves up to the second floor where more rooms overlook us. Beth raps on a door directly to our right and opens it unto a parlor converted into an invalid's bedroom.

As I said, I recognized her at a first sight: An enormous lizard sprawled on a loveseat bed. The sheets are pulled up under her leathery green arms and clutched by impossibly-long, webbed fingers. A cold unblinking reptile whose visage slowly resolves into that of a sickly green-tinged woman with porcelain skin, shiny black hair down to her shoulders and a long delicate nose.

When Elena has completed her transformation to the closest approximation of human she can manage, I turn my astonished eyes to see if Beth has witnessed the same spectacle.

What I see is an anxious sister presenting a beau for a sister's judgment.

"Well, here he is, dear. The one I've told you so much about," says Beth.

At that, the creature on the bed turns her gaze to me. Our eyes lock in a moment of mutual enmity. I see a reptilian, such as those I'd seen on the feed. I can see her eying me in the ruthless way an animal sizes up a threat to its survival.

But I haven't been a child of the modern age for all these years without learning how to be false. I force myself to approach the bed, eyes on the floor.

When I pick up her pale human hand, it is perfectly formed and cold.

"It's nice to meet you," I say, which is exactly 100 percent the opposite of what I feel.

"She says you don't like her. That you'll try to get rid of her."

It didn't take long for the animal sister to launch her crude attack. Subtle as I am, I've said nothing against her in these days since our first meeting. But Beth has picked up on a general lack of enthusiasm.

"It's just ... it's important that you understand. That she comes with me," says Beth. "I won't abandon my sister."

I look at her there, sticking out her defiant chin. So loyal and earnest, my heart goes to her. I look down at my hand, bandaged over the powdering skin and black mold where I touched that creature so briefly. I see Beth's unblemished arms that feed and clean the reptile. What is the nature of a magic that poisons one and absolves another? What is the depth of the deception that blinds and binds my Beth?

"What is her illness? You've never said," I say.

Beth has to stop and think for a moment, as people often do when they're sorting through memories tinged by magic.

"She's always been frail ... it's just gotten worse in these past years," she says finally.

"Is she your older sister?"

"No, we're twins," she says.

"Not identical," she adds after an awkward moment. "I mean, we're so different, of course."

"Yes, different," I say. I look at Beth's pink skin, golden hair, kind eyes. I remember the girl I met those dozen years ago, fresh and cheerful like a yellow jonquil in a spring garden. I passed her by then, knowing myself unworthy. Now I have greater need and fewer scruples and will gather her.

I compare her to the languid pale green thing whose black eyes brim with menace.

"Very different."

"What does that mean," she says, and in her defensive tone I hear her hardening against me, a little.

"It would be best if you could kill it. That would be the answer."

I've come to Roland for counsel. Of the few people I trust, Roland is the clearest in his recognition of the tides of magic sweeping about us.

"Because it will keep trying to kill you," says Roland, finishing his thought. "That's its nature."

We are down at the docks, drinking ale at a tavern whose balcony offers a sweeping view of the bay and the open ocean beyond a rock jetty below us.

I haven't seen Roland in years. He's a striking figure, tall and thin with shoulder-length salt-and-pepper hair and the piercing eyes of a gypsy. Roland is a fairie, I see that now, something I didn't quite grasp in those mad years together when he took me under his wing.

"I can't kill her," I sigh, burdened by the weight of my reality view. We're still embedded enough in the age of modernity for me to be sent to prison for murdering Beth's sister. And of course I would lose Beth.

"Can you tell me about it," I ask.

Roland pauses for a second, and then begins ticking his thoughts off on his fingers.

"What is there to know? If what you say is true, it's a reptilian. An animal with no human soul. It mimics human feeling to bind itself to caretakers. It will seek to maintain its hold on the host to the death. And it will defend itself against perceived threats."

"What is its nature?"

"It is a reptile. It shares the nature of the lower beings. It hates the cold, it's lazy. If you overfeed it, it becomes sluggish. ... If there is good news, it's that it's not smart. It's a low-order being."

"Why does it look so much like a woman? The ones you see on the view are full-grown lizard people."

Roland takes a pull on his tankard, and his eyes move across the ocean, as if looking for something there.

"It sounds like it's keeping itself in a half-existence, to maintain its connection with the sister. That would explain the invalid state, it's neither one nor the other."

"What if we were to bring out the lizard," I ask. "Would that break the bond with Beth? If she could see it as it truly is?"

Roland keeps his eyes on the ocean. After a long time, he looks at me and gives a wry shrug: Who knows?

We sit in silence, watching the sea gulls hang effortlessly in the air. I finally ask the question so hard to say, for everyone.

"What's happening to us?"

I wait until it feels like he's not going to

answer. I look down the length of the balcony to where a girl is sitting by herself, looking out at the cold blue sea. Her wavy brown hair is shredding in the afternoon wind; at times I can almost see through her.

"There is a feel of old magic returning," says Roland in a trance voice. "The gods of modernity have retired and the old folk are coming back. Ivy is spreading over the bombed-out church of reason. And the Christ is in retreat."

As I leave the tavern, I pass through a livestock show set up in the streets by the harbor. I don't remember there ever being a livestock event in this part of town, but it seems to makes sense now.

I'm wandering past the pens when a large pig comes running up and bites me in the outer thigh. Hard. The pig's owners pull him off me. But all their apologies don't lessen for one second the throbbing pain in my thigh.

At home in my basement, I survey the grapefruit-sized bruise on my thigh and the macerated flesh where the pig chewed me. My little black cat Mysterio joins me on the sofa, but is more interested in his pleasure than my pain.

The next day I make plans with Beth to visit Elena.

"You're right, we didn't get off on a good foot," I tell Beth – one of many little lies to keep things moving.

Elena is more human this evening. She is dressed in a pale blue bed jacket and propped up on a bank of pillows. With my eyes squinted I scan for signs of the lizard; but all I see is a pale dark-haired young woman. I set my bag by her bedside and pull forth a box of chocolates, careful not to touch her as I hand them over. Her eyes drift over the bandage on my hand and flicker in triumph – the touch of her has been slow to heal.

"You open them, Elizabeth," she says in husky voice that sounds like cigarettes and swamp water.

Beth offers me a chocolate and takes one herself. Elena, I see, has noticed the grocery bag next to her bed. Her nostrils flair, and for the first time this evening I see a lizard in the point of her nose and arched neck.

"So you will take my sister away," she says abruptly. "And how will you take care of her? What is it you do?"

I'm preparing my response when a smile turns the corner of my mouth. It suddenly strikes my fancy – a middle-aged fortune hunter explaining his motives to a parasitic lizard woman.

"Is it funny," shrieks Elena, sitting up in the bed. "You are stealing my only sister and you think it's funny!"

"Shush, darling," says Beth, rushing to the bedside. I wince as Beth takes Elena in her arms and lays her cheek upon her sister's hair.

"You've upset her," says Beth reproachfully. From her position in Beth's arms, Elena looks down into the bag at bedside and her nostrils again widen.

It's a charade, then, for the next few weeks as I pretend to get along with Elena while leaving my packages behind in her room.

One night I pounce. Beth needs to be taken. Some people do. A determined lover to force them through the door. We leave my Trojan horse offering to the reptile deity and climb the staircase to Beth's fine big room. We are swept up in my passion that precludes any precautions. As I make love I feel through the floor the angry vibrations of a large beast lumbering about below.

Elena never acknowledges the sacks of hamburger I leave at her bedside. But they must be disappearing because I never hear a word from Beth. Each visit I offer up a few false pleasantries and then it's upstairs for Beth and I. Leaving the animal to devour the raw meat and grow strong into her reptilian nature. So that Beth can finally perceive it and break free.

But even as her lizard side grows, so too, her magic. I am plagued by more attacks from the animal kingdom; more bad luck in general. Insect bites swell while money grows tight. Heavy strangers tread on my feet; carriage horses make me leap from their path, as do punks in sports cars.

It all comes to a head one chilly night when I am summoned to the brownstone. Elena has risen from her sickbed; she and Beth receive me in the formal receiving hall outside Elena's chambers. Elena is dressed in a bygone style from the old flickering analog projections, where women in square-shouldered gowns slinked about smoking cigarettes on long stems.

Beth is less manicured tonight. Her eyes are puffy and dull looking; she speaks as one who has lost a battle and now must honor her agreement to the victor. Even if she doesn't believe a word she is saying.

Beth tells me that I have raped her and that she will call the police unless I leave town immediately. She is pale and dressed in black, as if I have killed something within her. Which is 100 percent the opposite of what has happened, for I can see that I have quickened life in her womb. I can see it; the animal sister can see it; perhaps even Beth knows it from the slightly hunched way she holds herself.

I try to catch her eye. But the Beth I know is nowhere to be found in the averted gaze and droning voice asking me to leave.

Next to her, Elena is pulsing green. The illusion of humanity ripples and I have fleeting glimpses of a great lizard standing vertical before me; and then a woman in a dark green gown.

As Beth delivers her ultimatum, Elena signals me with a shift of her head; her white face and jet black hair, her green snout and wide leathery mouth. The triumphant lizard woman is signaling a door to me. A door I'd never noticed before on the other side of the hall. Go in, say Elena's bulging eyes. If you dare.

Beth's voice trails off as I cross the parlor and enter the room, which is a twin of the parlor used by Elena. It is a man's study, tall bookshelves and high ceiling. Curtains block the view from a large bay window nook. A gleaming oak desk is positioned before the window so the master might look out onto the street while doing his letters. A comfortable, affluent room.

A man is sitting at the desk with his back to me. He never moves as I enter the chamber, walking along one of the book-lined walls to reach the window nook.

His hands are placed sphinxlike on the desk, gripping the edge. He looks as if he had just sat down and was pulling his chair in. A well-groomed, elderly businessman settling in for his morning correspondence. And then never moving again.

Surely this is their father. It occurs to me that Beth and I have seldom spoken of him. Is there a geas about this, too? Relatives ignoring the stony transformation of a loved one?

From the look of him it's been several years since he got up from this desk. He's well-dusted, but the clothes have a stiff, weathered look. His desk is tidy with paper and pen; there's a fresh red rose in a bud vase and a glass of water left by a loving daughter.

The man's eyes are closed and his face has a neutral expression. The skin on his hand, when I touch it, has a slight crumbly texture of sandstone; a symptom that I've read will grow more pronounced as the years pass.

This man has resigned life, but is not dead. At least not according to the High Court, which has recently ruled that until a body shows signs of putrefaction, the person is legally considered to be alive. A true enough view of life in its limited way, I suppose. But a legal precedent that will not serve well the growing number of heirs anxious to inherit from their frozen benefactors.

Which means, as I think it through, this man's fortune will be tied to his care and maintenance for untold years to come; rather than passing to his daughters.

They're waiting for me as I close the study door behind me. Even though I no longer want a life with Beth, I will give her a chance to free herself from the parasite.

Your sister, I tell her, has been transformed

by magic. Her quality of cruelness, her lack of human feeling, has come to the fore. Destroying whatever human nature she had. Or never had.

I explain it to Beth, just as I have to you, dear reader. This inexplicable time of magic, how it's hard to think about it but changes are happening; people reverting to their intrinsic type, and more.

Your sister is a lizard woman, and you are her keeper.

I say this and other plain truths. And for a moment I believe I'm reaching Beth. She looks at Elena, puzzled.

Then Elena does a strange thing. She gives a little self-deprecating shrug as if to say 'Yes, I am a reptile, so what?'

It's all too much for Beth. She hits the reality wall where one cannot move forward. She runs to Elena's arms, is enfolded by her dark green sleeves.

From over Beth's head, Elena leers at me in triumph. My campaign to wrest Beth from her unnatural sister has failed.

Tell him, says Elena in her husky voice as she nudges Beth's head with her broad green nose.

Beth lifts her tear-streaked cheeks from Elena's bosom.

Even if what you say is true, says Beth, why is your reality more real than my own?

That is my last view of them as I walk past. The faint glow of Beth wrapped in the dark, absorbing arms of her sister.

And so I'm off. As soon as I've uploaded this final post, I'm leaving town. The doctor said I should head south, try to get some sunshine on the fungus attacking my privates. A peeling misery similar to the mold that so tenaciously afflicted my hand. The doctor says south, but I'm thinking north. Put some distance and cold weather between me and the power of the lizard woman's curses.

When I got home from my dismissal, yet another sad surprise awaited. I found my cat dead in the middle of the room. An inspection showed twin puncture wounds on one of his haunches. As I bent over my poor Mysterio, my cat eyes were drawn to something wiggling under the couch. An orange-and-red-banded tail twisting mindlessly after separation from its poisonous owner.

I can't stay here with some tailless killer creeping about. I can't keep having the dreams, night after night; the lizards running across my face and arms. Angry lizards on the attack, pouncing with needle-sharp teeth.

When you come from nothing, there's no one watching when you take a powder. I'm no hero, but I'm no fool, either. If I stay here I will die. It's the animal's nature. If it doesn't manage to kill me outright, it will drain me as it did the father.

I won't go alone. As a side project, I have been giving my healing ministrations to the girl at the bar; the one so near to fading, as I sensed that afternoon with Roland. I have brought her back from the brink with my touch, and worked my magic on her womb, as well. This effusion of fertility is a baffling turn of fate after a solitary life.

Shawna will go with me, more as servant than companion; for a while. And my attention, poor though it be, will feed her diminished soul. And then she will have a baby to anchor her in this world.

I'm posting this account on my PersonalView feed in the hope someone will record it and set it aside for my child. If Elena allows it to survive. And that my child may know it has a sibling, somewhere, from the woman, Shawna.

This is a letter from your father, my sons or daughters. It is the truest story I can tell from a man who knows many ways to be false. Perhaps we may meet some day if the fates allow. More likely this is all you will have from me.

I could tell you my name, but it is not the name your mothers know me by; nor the name I will use tomorrow. Remember, rather: I come from nothing. When you come from nothing, anything is gravy.

In these times of change, my dears, may your eyes be quick and your feet agile. Be light, my little ones, be nimble.

The Night Ronnie Fagged Out!

When he was a boy, Ronnie's favorite comic book character was a hero who wielded powers of concealment and self-protection. Her name was the Invisible Girl and she could both disappear, as billed, and cast protective force shields. In the comics these force fields were drawn as semi-translucent white domes; with a dotted line depicting concentration from her forehead to the inner circumference of her invisible wall. You could see her, and anyone with her, inside the bubble; but in muted colors, as if she were in a different, less-vital, dimension.

Later on they souped up her powers and gave her feminist attitude. But in the beginning, Invisible Girl was a classic wimpy girl sidekick. She got kidnapped a lot, and her powers were mostly unsuccessful to the task. She might spy on Dr. Doom or The Puppet Master and gain valuable information. And then be tripped up by sleeping gas or a dog barking to reveal her unseen presence. Her shields would mostly provide only momentary protection before crumbling under an enemy's onslaught.

Given this feminine identification with passive attributes, you might be picturing Ronnie as some precious Dickensian sissy boy in knee pants, with pale skin and delicate golden locks; quick to tears, cosseted by his mother and battered by a universe of schoolyard bullies.

But in truth, Ronnie was a vigorous boy. Wanting to hide inside your own little fortress is a wish dear to many, many boys of all persuasions. Ronnie grew up with older brothers and learned to claw for the things he wanted, just as any other child.

It was this very aspect of, if not exactly butchness, passable masculinity that gave Ronnie varied options later in life. Landed him, some would say, in the drama about to unfold.

We join Ronnie – all grown up with a wife and kid – on an ordinary Sunday morning in his household on Hastings-on-Hudson, one of many comfortable suburbs along the Metro North train line flowing out of New York City.

Our scene begins on the first floor of the 3-bedroom, 2 1/2-bath Shaker Style bungalow on a corner lot her parents helped them buy. Gotta hand it to her, Peggy has successfully married a French country kitchen with a New England beach cottage den – browns and greens in the kitchen married with white wainscoted walls and navy blue woven fabrics in the sunken family room. It sounds like it wouldn't work together, but it somehow does.

Ronnie is sitting at the oversized – for the three of them – farmer's table, working on his first cup of coffee. He's wearing the royal blue terry towel bathrobe Peggy got him for Christmas. Oh brother, did she match his robe to the downstairs decor? Ronnie's wishing he'd brought his slippers down from upstairs. His bare feet are cold on the over-sized terra cotta tiles in the kitchen. And he's more than a little hung over.

Ronnie is trying to pull himself together after an unusual night of carousing. As he scans the headlines, head propped up in hands, our protagonist has no clue of the dangers awaiting him. The fabric of his universe will hang in the balance, as he deals with the fearsome consequences of ... The

Night Ronnie Fagged Out!

Enter the sidekick. Ronnie's 12-year-old daughter Miranda shuffles down the stairs and joins him at the kitchen table. She fetches her smart phone from the basket where they make her leave it each night. Ronnie and Peggy are a little old fashioned about the whole social media, networking, Internet thing for their little girl. Miranda has a cellphone for communicating while she's away from them; but the rest of it, the texting and sexting and God knows what else – that stays downstairs until she's older. At least while she's under their roof.

Without a word to him, Miranda huddles over her phone.

"Good morning," he says, but his ironic tone goes unacknowledged.

There was a time when Miranda was Ronnie's little pal. Co-conspirators plotting minor anarchies against the Peggy regime. Miranda was what made it all worthwhile. He could look at her antics, her Dora the Explorer phase, the awful ballet recitals and softball games, and know, really know in his heart, that he'd made the best choice with his life.

But now Miranda is all transition: blemishes and braces and chest bumps. And prickly attitude; she doesn't collaborate with her dad anymore. She has, much too early to Ronnie's mind, slid into the generic Disney Channel diva phase. He does blame the media, all these little girls on TV with pointy nails and painted lips, carrying designer purses and tossing off withering putdowns. So beyond their years, little sexualized bitches, and now they want to recruit Miranda, too. Ronnie can only hope he'll see his daughter again at the other end of the self-involved tunnel she's entered.

Ronnie turns back to the newspaper. Between waves of nausea, he's been trying to wade through a story about the Hadron collider in Switzerland. He has never understood what the God particle is. It sounded like a small piece of a molecule; but what made that godly? In another few years better microscopes would prove that the piece of molecule was made up of even smaller particles. It would be like the time the Fantastic Four chased Dr. Doom into the microverse – worlds within worlds.

"Lisa texted me. She says 'your dad really fagged out last night.'"

"What?"

Miranda turns the face of her phone to him, illustrating for her dull father the concept of a text message: A brief missive sent from one phone-holding person to another to convey key information or emotional status.

"It says 'your dad really fagged out last night.' That's all it says. What did you do," she asks accusingly.

Fagging out.

Ronnie can feel his face freezing up as his thoughts flash back to his freshman year in college. Smoking dope for the first time with his dorm mates. And then seeing one or more of them recoil in revulsion after he opened his mouth to say something.

It seemed the marijuana uncaged some lisping, sissy, inner demon that seldom saw the light of day. Ronnie was completely unaware of this emergence, this transformation – except for what he saw in the faces of his friends. It took multiple hazy episodes for Ronnie to accept the connection; deeply painful moments when some half-stoned alpha teen's face would contort in disgust. One moment he was on equal footing with his peers; the next he was a pariah.

Others in his college circle ignored these Liberace unicorn moments.[1] They were worse, letting him go on and on embarrassing himself. Never saying anything, but surely laughing behind his back. He eventually quit smoking in group situations. Ronnie retired weed to the crowded field of his hidden pleasures.

It might be argued that rare moments that surprise us, lapses when we do or think something uncensored and unfiltered, are important beacons of self-illumination; clues to be studied and acted upon. Harken to the behemoths rising from the depths to roil the surface you with occasional glimpses of your primitive, authentic self.

But in Ronnie's case, any curiosity to look at this raw data from the psyche was crushed by his paralyzing fear of deviating from the norm.

"Daddy was a little drunk. You know it was a big night."

Miranda frowns and turns back down to her phone, tapping out keys.

"What are you saying," says Ronnie. "Don't respond to that. When people are rude just ignore them."

With a snort of derision, Miranda gets up from the table and throws herself onto the blue canvas sofa of the adjoining family room. He hears a faint tap-tap-tap.

With his daughter out of sight, Ronnie feels his facial muscles relax. He begins reviewing the past night for chinks in his hetero armor.

There had been the company dinner in

Manhattan, where his ad agency celebrated a big award for a cosmetics campaign spearheaded by Ronnie. Ronnie's ability to drink the Kool-Aid, to make lemonade from lemons, had made him a natural for the ad biz. Last night was a night of triumph, a coup. Did it go to his head and make him careless? Was there a disruption in his hologram of a happily-married family man?

They'd stopped off at that West Village piano bar recommended by Gale, his work colleague. Lisa's parents, Rob and Joan, had met up with them for a drink after their own night on the town. That must be it. What had Lisa overheard her parents saying about him?

It's at this point, dear reader, when Ronnie's sluggish thoughts start to pick up the pace. The coffee is kicking in; so is a little panic. All his forgotten college drama, being unmasked and unmanned, finds new purchase in Ronnie's bilious thoughts.

What was the name of the bar? Marie's Crisis, a little cellar of a place. They had a couple drinks and sang show tunes for Christ's sake. Some "Grease," some Rodgers and Hammerstein. They didn't even stay that long.

With no apparent lapses coming to mind, Ronnie reluctantly turns to his personal greatest hits of swishiness. The boozy interpretative dance he'd once performed at a bar to a song with the refrain "I'm only human." The college cast party for "Gypsy," where he and that girl had bumped and grinded to "Gotta Have a Gimmick." His hips hitting the mark as he sang with an "uh," and an "uh," and an "uh, uh, uh."

There had been a common theme to those

nadirs – a lot of alcohol and weed. And all before he was married. But last night?

Guiltily, Ronnie's mind replays the moments outside the dive bar, smoking half a joint with Gale. Shotgunning the smoke, shooting it in a stream back and forth to hoard the weed. Almost like kissing, he'd gotten a little hard.

Gale. Somehow Gale's gayness had rubbed off on him last night. But how?

Thump!

Ronnie stands up in time to see Miranda deliver a second savage kick to the rounded armrest of the sofa where she's sprawled. He steps down from the orange kitchen tiles to the whitewashed pine planks of the den. He peers down at his daughter from the backside of the sofa. She looks up hostilely at him from her bower, her smart phone face down upon her insignificant bosom.

"Is it everywhere?" he asks, trying to smile. "Is it so terrible?"

"You don't understand," she says with all the passion of a hurt child.

"Sweetie," he says after a moment, "there are mean people out there. Some want to be mean just for the sake of being mean, and some just get swept up in it. ... You're so young, everything seems huge to you. But you have to be tougher."

"Imagine you have a protective shield," he says, holding his palms out to touch the inner walls of a dome. "And nothing can get inside."

After enduring a stare-down worthy of an Old West gunslinger, Ronnie retreats.

Back at his table with a fresh cup, Ronnie finds himself thinking of his wedding day. Standing at the altar in front of 150 of mostly Peggy's guests, holding her gloved hand and trembling as he said his vows.

When I was a child, I spoke as a child. I saw as a child and understood as a child. But when I became a man, I put away childish things.

Yes, reader, he'd really gone there. He'd meant it, too. He was putting aside the indiscretions of his youth: Circling that park in his car at night, those public restrooms. The underground network of repressed lust. Ronnie knew the bargain he was making, or thought he did. He didn't want to be one of those guys. He wanted a family. What was youth for, anyway, but to bind oneself to impossible promises? To love and cherish for a lifetime. Who could do that? To never change, to never grow, to never want something you never imagined you could want.

And he'd been true to his promise, mostly. There's been that episode in the Sheraton sauna on the business trip to San Antonio. A few similar lapses, marked by extreme fear, guilt and excitement on his part; and no emotional connection to the other party in the furtive trysts.

Gale.

Ronnie punches in the passcode to his smart phone and calls up his work e-mail. After an intermittent download resembling his jumbled mental state, he sifts through his inbox for any word from Gale about last night. He ruefully notes his own disappointment at not finding anything.

Why would Gale log on at 4 a.m. to send a follow-up note about the evening? That was something teenagers did; or lovers.

They'd gotten close working on the cosmetics campaign for a famous door-to-door line. He was the words and Gale the art. Gale was new to the agency. A quintessential New York City art director; good looking, well dressed, charming. Thick brown eyebrows perfectly manicured; out and proud with a gay man's gym body.

Working together on the campaign, they became confidantes. Gale would occasionally share details of his conquests with Ronnie, who played the bored married voyeur role. Pleading for vicarious details of the single co-worker's love life. Married 14 years, I got nothing, Ronnie would say.

In a burst of conspiratorial camaraderie, Ronnie once asked Gale if he was a top or a bottom.

Who wants to know, Gale had said coolly, looking Ronnie in the eye intently, like a pirate. And then a flash of his rogue's smile as he remembered the rules – he was gay, but Ronnie was straight.

That's how it worked for Ronnie, back in the day. You could think whatever you liked, but if you spoke, you played by Ronnie's ground rules. He was straight; any question or challenge would trigger a freeze-out. Like one of Susie's force fields, but icy cold.

Occasionally through his youth, some intrepid soul – his mother, for one, or some aggressive girl who couldn't believe he didn't want her goodies – might rub their hands on the surface of the igloo. Clear a porthole and peer inside for the person amid the icy mist. But the glass would quickly cloud over.

Versatile, Gale had said lustily, waggling his eyebrows.

Not that Ronnie had any illusion that Gale thought he was straight. Gale knew his secret, in the way fairies knew each other. Ronnie had even departed from his 'Think whatever you want' policy to occasionally, almost, not quite, acknowledge his precious secret.

Was Gale flirting with him last night when he stepped in close to blow smoke in Ronnie's mouth? Or was he just having fun with the closet case from work who so obviously had a crush on him? Trying to stir up some trouble in the happy household, like a mischievous sprite.

Or, more likely, had Ronnie projected all the Byzantine turning of his mind onto Gale, who was just being friendly?

By now Ronnie's thoughts are at full boil. He feels a great heaviness descending upon his shoulders. It shouldn't be this hard, he thinks to himself. Getting through your life. It shouldn't be this hard. You try to celebrate one high point in your life and it turns into a debacle.

Where was Peggy? She didn't usually stay abed this long. Was she upstairs packing his things? Had he finally been exposed to her in a way that allowed no backtracking? The basic incompatibility revealed?

Would he be cast out? She and Miranda would keep the house, of course. Where would he go? A tiny studio in Manhattan? They didn't have the money for that. Unless he moved to the Bronx or some other frightening hinterland.

With a collapsing feeling of despair, Ronnie turns his eyes on the staircase up to their bedrooms. Up the brown walnut steps to the carpeted second floor, where his wife and partner could very well be making plans to exile him from the comfortable life – he saw that now – that he had been dream-walking through.

Was this the day? The day his life would

surely change?

Much as we might wish otherwise, life is not the comics. Life is not ray guns and rings of power or super villains inked in four-color dot-matrix printing. Disasters are flatter in real life. Catastrophes are slower in coming. There are warning tremors before the earthquake.

So it is with the dull thud of anti-climax that Peggy finally comes downstairs and fixes everything. For she is, after all, the greatest of super heroes – the Wife and Mother.

Peggy takes in Miranda's distress at a glance. With the seasoned skill of a Cape Cod oyster shucker, she pries out the salient details. She gets Joan on the phone for damage control. Here's the spin: Boy, Ronnie sure was drunk last night. Poor guy, he's been working so hard and finally cut loose. And what about that co-worker? Boy, some guys just can't take no for an answer. ... And, don't know if you know, but your Lisa posted something on those sites, about Ronnie. ... Oh, I don't want to go into it, just ask her to take it down ... But really, it wasn't Ronnie so much as the co-worker, totally out of bounds ... You will? Thanks so much ... It's just Miranda is so sensitive ... These kids ...

Oh good one, Peg. When in doubt, throw the gay under the bus. Make the gay the aggressor, the predator. An oldie but a goodie, still effective!

After settling Miranda's hash as best she can, Peggy sits next to Ronnie at the big table. She idly picks up the design section. Peggy can't quite give him a greeting yet; it's a delicate matter to make up over a fight that never happened.

The thing is, Peggy agrees with Ronnie's

assessment that he'd be no good in the gay world. Particularly now, with his thinning hair and love handles. Even when he was young, and handsome in that fleeting Yankee way, it was no good. He wasn't tough enough for that lifestyle, that brutal, lonely lifestyle. She married him as much to rescue him, as to cement him into the future she wanted.

There's one thing, though, rankling usually-steadfast Peggy. She's seen his eye wander when some shirtless Adonis goes by. She can live with that, if the Vatican can. It's okay to have impulses as long as you don't act on them.

No, the unexpected burr under her saddle, is something different: The emotional current that Joan noticed and blabbed about in front of her daughter.

Ronnie had seemed so happy last night. With that man, that Gale from work. The way they laughed together, describing the absurdities of their workplace. And then the piano player doing "Carousel" and Ronnie and that man leading the bar.

Longing to tell you, but afraid and shy. I'd let my golden chances, pass me by.

Loyal and well-trained as he was, Ronnie had directed his singing to her. But it hadn't been for her.

She never got to see that side of Ronnie. Giddy and carefree and silly. It discomfited her. The easy spark of attraction between Ronnie and that man, so different from the forced heartiness of their own sex life.

She had seen this rare side of her husband; and so had, apparently, Joan. That cunt.

Ronnie has watched in admiration as Peggy tackled the Miranda crisis. That was his Peggy; powerful, decisive, cutting to the core. She was a builder, a problem solver. Like a mother bird she flitted around the nest, pecking at interlopers. He had delegated everything to her, and she had spun gold from it.

He'd gotten infected by his daughter's pre-teen drama. He can see that, now. Vibrating on the same pitch, the same shocked despair over peer rejection; echoing his early stoner rebuffs. The naked vulnerability of trying to understand why people didn't like you.

Peggy brings over the coffee pot and fills his cup. When their gaze meets, for the first time that morning, she rolls her eyes wearily. Ostensibly over Miranda's histrionics; but also as a symbol of the mantra that keeps their family ship afloat: Don't rock the boat.

As he stirs artificial sweetener into his cup, Ronnie notes his terror – yes, that was the word, a hell of a thing on a Sunday morning – easing into a faint melancholia. A vague disappointment that life will go on as before, after all his bracing for the upheaval.

It occurs to Ronnie. Maybe the real fear was not that he would lose her; but that she would never let him go.

That's all the time for today, dear reader.

As the Invisible Man and Super Mom think their separate thoughts, is that a fissure we see cracking between them? Is this the beginning of the end for the dynamic pair? Will Peg cast off this strange uncertainty about the ethics of being Ronnie's ... jailer? Will Ronnie continue to feel let down that his life hasn't changed? What about Gale, the coworker – friend or villain?

And will vulnerable Miranda survive the cruelty of her peers, who even now are ganging up on her with cyber taunts about her own sexuality?

Check back next time for further installments of ... The Night Ronnie Fagged Out!

[1] **unicorn moment** *noun*

A.: spontaneous action or thought that might illuminate unconscious wishes or attitudes

B.: rare insight that catches one off guard

C.: silly, embarrassing behavior

Far Away, And In Someone Else's Ass

This is it, you think. This is the night you get AIDS.

It doesn't seem to matter too much. It will be a relief, won't it? All the panic of your 20s, 30s, 40s, sweating out the tests, fretting over every bruise and swollen gland; you can't seem to spark it up. You are mentally exhausted from the war. Drained by the passion-sapping negotiations: 'I'll do this, but I won't do that.' Weary of inventing yourself as a condom top when you want it, too: A big hard cock shooting warm cum up your ass. You fought the good fight, but now you can lay it all down in surrender.

Haven't you been chasing it, anyway, in your usual muddled way? Lowering your standards through the years as the quarry gets harder to bag. Less discerning as you realize that magic you've been waiting for isn't going to happen. Cranking your tired libido with depravity. What does it matter? It's just going to be you: Old, older, oldest. It all goes flushing down the pipes tonight. That thing swirling in the bowl? That's you, newly 50 and loathsome, no fool like an old fool, finally attaining the fatal fuck-up.

You're a writer, describe the scene from the start. Capture every detail. You'll want to punish yourself with this memory, again and again.

Your eyes open. You're lying on a bed. Did you pass out? You look at an etched glass fixture on the ceiling. You feel nauseated and strangely inert. A moldy air conditioner rattles in the corner, muffling the traffic noise from Eighth Avenue. It's your hotel room. The nylon comforter under you feels scratchy on your skin; it's a blob of turquoise in your side vision. There's the little TV sitting on the shabby brown dresser. And the little round walnut veneer table and two chairs, with the plastic ice bucket and bottle of Jack Daniels.

Downstage left is the costar of this seedy passion play: The Puerto Rican hustler currently sifting through your duffle bag. He's a fine piece of rough trade. That was what you wanted, wasn't it? Buzzed hair and brown skin, tattoos and muscles; his shirt is off and his pants are open, his half-hard cock dangles out.

Seeing the cock perks you up. You have sucked that cock. Ah, the delicious moment when your lips open for a big hard cock. It's a moment of joy, yes it is. Look at your little boy now, Daddy. But even in this guilty rapture, you can't let go. There are rules, there are always rules.

Safer sex tips for oral. If you taste pre-cum, back off. Squeeze the base of the cock and milk the pre-cum out. Wipe it off the cock slit with your hand. Then suck it some more. Don't let him come in your mouth; shield your eyes when the young ones shoot.

The hustler rummages through your pants, finds the wallet. Why are your pants over there? There goes the cash, and your credit card. You try to protest but only moan. He comes over to the bed and looks down on you. This one is all-Bronx; homely, when you get past the beefcake. He has crude tattoos on his upper chest and shoulders, like a child's doodles. He'd had a nice smile in the bar, that notorious Times Square bar. He let you feel his cock under the table while you chatted; nice fat cock.

The hustler leans over and dribbles down a line of spit. It splashes in your left eye and runs down the side of your face. He takes his cock in hand and bats your face, making himself hard. He puts one knee on the bed and mounts your mouth, face fucks you contemptuously. You try to cooperate but receive the thrusts passively. He goes too deep and you gag. Stomach acid burns your throat. He pulls out and stalks over to the table.

Something has made the hustler angry. He fixes himself a Jack and Coke. He fishes a small pipe from his jacket and loads it. Is it crack, crystal meth? Watching the hustler smoke up makes you think of your own modest debauchery. This is your birthday present to yourself, a sleazy weekend in Manhattan. Get drunk, smoke some joints. See the "Streetcar" revival with that TV actress you like. Fondle some go-go boys. Jerk off in a video booth. "Play" in the big city, be a "naughty boy." The juvenile vocabulary of the aimless gay man.

The hustler puts the pipe down and stares. He's high.

Safer sex and drugs. Don't do drugs if they make you lose control. Don't drink too much if you can't handle it. Don't lose control. Keep the big picture in view. Your health is worth more than one peak experience.

Your thoughts clear a bit. You remember bringing the hustler to your room, past the disapproving guard in the lobby. He fixed drinks at the little table. He insisted on that, like a straight guy who needs alcohol before he'll let a faggot touch him. Hot!

You remember now. You set your empty glass on the table and slid over to kneel before the hustler. Nuzzling his crotch, unbuttoning him, taking it out. Time for the poppers, in one nostril, the other.

Your blood vessels expand, your skin feels warm and tingly. A nice big cock, getting hard and fat in your pussy mouth. Happy birthday to me, happy birthday to me. You feel rebellious pride in yourself, acting so scandalous and horny at your age. You're alive, not like all those sleepwalking married guys. The balls, you want to suck the balls. You pull the jeans past his ass and down to his knees.

That's when you see them. The lymph nodes, twin paths of stepping stones running along the hustler's inner thighs.

It's a common cocksucker practice. Suck any dick you want as long as the owner looks healthy. The minute you see a hint he's positive, shun him like a leper.

That's what made the hustler mad. Being rejected by a disgusting old queen. Perfectly understandable. But how did you end up on this bed, so limp? How did you end up here. That's a good one.

You moan and the hustler rouses. He comes to the foot of the bed and lifts your legs, jerking your body towards him. Your sad little penis hangs upside down as he positions himself for the fuck.

Safer sex tips for anal. Be the top in one-night stands and anonymous scenes. Wear a condom. Don't get fucked by strangers. When you do get fucked, make him wear a condom. Condoms break. Even with the condom, make him agree to pull out before he comes. If he won't agree, don't let him fuck you. If he agrees but you don't believe him, don't let him fuck you. Don't get fucked by strangers.

The hustler's dick is soft. He can't get it in. With an angry snort he drops your legs and goes over to his coat. When he comes back, he has a knife in his hand.

Final thoughts on safer sex. Remember, even with all your precautions, it's still a numbers game. Don't stay too long, don't sink too low. Don't get trapped in the hunt …

With the point of his knife, the hustler begins scratching designs on your chest and stomach. His face has a look of concentration like a child taking a spelling test. Oh God!

With a druggy smile, the hustler draws the knife along his own abdomen, catching drops of red on the edge of the blade. Then the knife drops out of sight. The blood! Not the blood! He flicks the knife and a drop hits your eye. The room explodes in red, the hustler suddenly horned and demonic.

… Not every gay is your brother. Being gay warps some people, makes them self-centered and dangerous. Understand them. Protect yourself …

The hustler is hard. You feel his cock slide in as if from far away, and in someone else's ass. He smiles at you, such white teeth, as he pumps his hips lasciviously. Look at me, *Papí.* He hoists one of your ankles on his shoulder as he pushes in deeper. With the knife in his right hand, he continues his drawing game. My blood, your blood.

… Don't let sex become the main thing. Believe in love, be worthy of it. Don't become solitary, nurture friendships. Keep looking for your purpose. Don't let the animal in you rule the human. Maintain balance. In all things moderation. Be accountable for your actions …

The hustler drops the knife and takes your other ankle upon his shoulder. He pumps faster and your stomach fat jiggles. He spits on you again. Blood or sweat is trickling down your side onto the comforter. They might charge you if it's stained.

Your panic ebbs as the hustler nears climax. Your thoughts come to you dull and distant. This is it, you think. This is the night.

It doesn't seem to matter too much.

... Love yourself. Respect yourself. Don't give in to despair. Don't give up hope.

Gypsy Prince Of The Steam Room

I first glimpse him in the mist. The
eucalyptus-scented clouds part, heaven opens its
portals. My heart skips a beat, so stunned, so
awestruck am I by this dark angel in the sauna.
Adonis in a white cotton towel; wiry muscles, shaggy
damp locks, a noble profile. A rogue, a pirate king, a
gypsy prince.

The heavy glass door swings shut behind me
and I approach with due reverence this godling exile
from Olympus. I settle near him – not too near! – on
the slick tiles. My heightened senses take in every
detail; the condensation dripping from the ceiling,
the diffuse glow leaching through the fogged glass.
Heavy bass from the disco version of "MacArthur
Park" thumps through the walls, accented by the
occasional clang of dropping dumbbells.

It is a magic moment. And opportune, for we
are alone. I must be about the hunt. I adjust my
towel alluringly, suck in my gut and throw back my
shoulders to keep my chests from cupping in that
unappealing way. If only he would look up, he would
see everything in my eyes. All the lonely years, the
meaningless encounters – some of them in this very
steam room. He would see that, yes, but more: The
beautiful youth grown middle-aged and sad, the
bright embers of his heart gone cold and ashy.
Waiting for the hero, waiting for Prometheus to bring
fire down from the heavens and relight this torch.

But his gaze stays down, fixed upon his
magnificent feet, strong like a dancer's. And his
calves, supple and brown, fringed in robust, curly

hairs growing dense upon his thighs – Oh!

I must be bold, take a page from the immortal bard: "There is a tide in the affairs of men, which taken at the flood, leads on to fortune: Omitted, all the voyage of their life is bound in shallows and miseries."

I will slide across the shallows and miseries, dropping all pretenses – and possibly my towel.

And then, wouldn't you know it? A shadow darkens our glass door, light and noise puncture our interlude. In comes a horrible poof, a gray-chested, spindly-legged ancient. This withered bird gives me the briefest of glances before flying across the room, practically landing in my prince's lap. Before I can twist the poof's head off – it's the only way to kill them – the door opens again. Two slanty-eyed elves, chattering in their elfish tongue.

The party's over when the elves show up. No self-respecting mortal will commit indiscretions before their inhuman gaze. And once the elves get a whiff of mischief, they're in for the count. Can't scrape them off with a spatula.

The door opens again. A big, fat, hairy ogre.

I lose my prince amid the onslaught of monsters and evil fae. I'm not sure how he slips out. I fume as I peek for him in the shower stalls and locker room aisles. First meetings are supposed to be magical, don't you think? Beautiful moments, so rare, so easily ruined. There's always some desperate beast horning in, lifting its gnarly leg to piss on your happiness.

I watch for him after that. The gypsy is in my thoughts when I wake up, when I go to sleep. It surprises me to feel this way, so smitten. I up my modest exercise regime. I am realistic. Perhaps it was for the best that our first moment was interrupted. Gives me a chance to work on some things. While I am a remarkably well-preserved handsome man, there is a little too much of me these days. But nothing some abdominal crunches and a low-carb diet can't fix in a twinkle. I will be ready, better, for my next chance.

Weeks go by, and I despair. He was some tourist passing through the Big Apple, gone now forever. He was just a wish, he will just fade away.

And then I see him again. It is a Thursday night, an hour before closing. A chilly rain outside has left the gym empty. As before, my prince is in the corner of the steam room. Leaning forward like Rodin's Thinker, elbow on knee, chin on hand.

I must strike fast. I walk in, stand in front of my prince. I must see his face straight on, his eyes, his soul! I will break the rules of propriety, the silence of strangers.

"How's it going," I croak. How this gypsy affects me, transforming me into a gawky adolescent.

As my prince lifts his face, a raucous scream bursts through the steam room. Behind me in the alcove by the door, two sharp-tongued harpies are laughing.

"Too sad," says one, as her twin screeches.

The door opens and in comes a giant, his black bulk filling the doorway. Behind him is a zombie, gray skin stretched tight across sunken cheeks and skeletal limbs.

When I turn back, my prince is looking down again. I study his thick black hair, memorizing him, loving him. He has a strip of leather tied around his left wrist. A swirl of black hair adorns his navel, widening into a triangle that disappears beneath his towel – Oh!

The sauna continues to fill up with vile creatures and my gypsy slips away.

The winter days grow shorter. I begin to haunt the sauna. My skin grows red and scaly from steaming. I learn to turn the temperature dial down as I enter to allow myself longer time on patrol, waiting like faithful Narcissus by his pond. I look up each time the door opens, my face alive with longing, only to have my hopes dashed.

I can't seem to lose any weight, either.

Just when I am losing hope again, I see him. As before, in the steam room. And again, we are interrupted by ogres and ancients and walking dead; all the faces of the lonely, grasping horde.

I begin to distrust my senses, my reality. How is he able to escape each time, slipping out of that one-door room? Is he real, or am I drifting Ophelia-like into madness? Is he some fairy prince casting a stupefying glamour in his wake? I have yet to see his face straight on, or make him see me. It is as if we move in slightly separate dimensions.

In desperation, I consult my hag. It's a risky gambit, for Serena is under the sway of a new oracle and prone to interrupt with her teacher's insights. Serena dyes her hair black and wears big round plastic frames, going for a Jackie O look that sounds fun but doesn't really work for her. Like many hags, she is queenier than a queen. She likes to refer to us as "Triple Fs" – fat, forty and fabulous – which I find unnecessary. I think Serena sees her role in our friendship as the grounder, the balloon buster. We meet at the Starbucks on Eighth Avenue and 16th

Street. She sips her Chai tea with infusion of ginger and listens intently as I tell her of my elusive gypsy prince.

"Oh honey," she says, patting my hand. "You've got it bad, haven't you?"

I nod, a sudden lump in my throat. I am 12 again, tender and vulnerable.

"Honey, when people aren't interested, they pretend not to notice. They see you, but pretend not to see you, so then they don't have to reject you. It's just easier, you know?"

I try to tell Serena that I really don't believe he has ever actually seen me. Our eyes have never met, strange as it seems. But then she begins to quote the oracle on destructive, self-replicating patterns, and working on yourself first, blah, blah, blah.

"Oh, honey," she says, as I extricate myself from our *tête-a-tête*, "You've always been so dramatic. It's the writer in you."

That's the thing about Serena. Amidst her blather there are usually some useful kernels. As you surely have noticed by now, I am one of those rare cultured souls who express themselves sublimely in prose. And perhaps I would have found worldly success at it, if I hadn't also been a seeker of beauty. My life, my deepest impulses and energies have been directed in the pursuit of beauty. In the bars, the Internet, the gay streets of Manhattan. What some might call a one-night stand is to me a life's work, an unending quest for perfection. Searching, sampling, separating the wheat from the chaff. Like the alchemist, I struggle to make gold from base material. Undaunted by dwindling returns, I march downward into ruin with head high and shoulders back to avoid the cupping chests. Nameless in this tale, call me Don Quixote, dreaming his impossible dream. I am Lancelot, seeking his Holy Grail.

Maybe, as Serena says, it is my writer's power, my sense of drama that allows me to recognize this opportunity. Perhaps there is some life lesson here. Some karmic obstacle to finally vault over on my path to nirvana. At long last I am presented with my perfect beauty, my heart's desire. I will part the dimensions, seize a new destiny. Nothing precious is won easily. At the fateful hour, the hero must be heroic. I must conquer the legions of evil trying to separate me from my gypsy, my Ganymede, my Tadzio.

"Pop that pimple and move on, Marty," calls out Serena. "Get over it, ya big drama queen."

A light snow is falling as I enter the gym. I smoked a joint as I walked over, and my heart is racing from the magic herb's power. I undress in the locker room, skipping exercise to take up my post in the steam room. Somehow I have a feeling tonight is the night. I have taken that drug to make myself fuller under the towel. You know which one I mean. I will ply all my manly charms to capture my prince's attention.

The steam is scalding and pungent. I put my hands in front of me as I step blindly forward. My heart jumps when I see him in the corner. We are alone. Trembling, I settle next to him, boldly close, my towel loose. Slowly I move my knee, further, further, until it touches his, ever so slightly. The steam is so dense I can barely see him. Miraculously, he doesn't pull his knee back.

As I sit there trying to bring my breath under

control, I hear a strange noise, like a horse whinnying. The far wall of the sauna seems to be giving way. I have the sense of a forest in the mist, a slight hill leading down to a campfire, a wagon and horses. A traveling show. A gypsy caravan.

I feel my prince's knee pull away and he stands up. Strangely, he is no longer bare-chested but dressed in some loose shirt of rough cloth, with pants tucked into boots. From behind, I see a hoop of gold in his left ear. He is stepping into the misty wall, into the forest. I hear the horses again, and singing. There is a smell of wet leaves.

With an animal reflex completely separate from my transfixed consciousness, I grab his hand, turning him back to me, in the sauna.

At long last I have my look in his face. And it is all that I dreamed of, more handsome and magnificent then I imagined: White teeth, strong fine nose, and black eyes. Black eyes of the Medusa, freezing me, killing me with their complete and utter disgust. They reflect myself as he sees me, old and abhorrent. They pierce me with a revulsion that goes like a knife into my chest, twisting painfully in my heart. He spits out some word in European, wrenching his hand away. He turns and goes down the hill. The mists swirl around me as I grab my chest, falling forward, tumbling down a leaf-strewn ditch, blackness.

"Are you coming to?"

I open my eyes, squinting at a bright white light overhead. I am lying on the floor. From this vantage point I can see the porcelain and pipe underbellies of a row of sinks.

A circle of faces above me. A vise-like grip

87

around my dead heart. There is a towel under my head, and a wet washcloth on my forehead. Like Dorothy, after she's gone black and white again.

"Are you all right? You fainted in the steam room. And you have a cut on your head."

It is one of the young people from the front desk; the ones who never stop talking to each other as they take your card and scan it.

Tears well as I recall the look in the gypsy's eyes.

"Just rest easy. An ambulance is on the way."

Behind the assistant manager, more faces. Trolls.

"They found you on the floor, in the corner. You're lucky someone came in. This one went for help, and this one gave you CPR." The manager gestures at two trolls, who nod and smile encouragingly, baring huge twisted yellow teeth.

If I could die right now, I would. Instead, I recline on the bathroom floor, looking at polka dots of gum pressed into the particle board sink counter.

The pain in my chest throbs, and I moan. My prince is gone, the spell broken. I will spend the rest of my life waiting for my beauty, my gypsy. My angel, my destroyer. But he will never come.

And worse yet, adding insult to injury, I owe my life to the trolls. They breathed their foul breath into me, steadied my faltering heart with their hairy hands. Pulled me down into the cavernous depths, made me one of their own. I can feel the warts bursting forth on my face, the hair springing up between my knuckles. In my decisive hour, I am rejected. I take my place with the vanquished, another cursed beast in the legion of ugly and unwanted.

Is this my karmic lesson?

Or is there something more? Is there some bright side to my descent into the underworld? Is there some positive aspect to this crushing spiritual debacle that has left me prone and drained of any will to push on? Is there some way to pluck redemption from this watery Waterloo? Has something transformative happened that in my present state I'm too crushed to appreciate?

I will consult my hag.

Or better, perhaps, a personal injury wizard.

Buying It

The ad said "eastern European," which appealed to him. Along with that beautiful ass shot. Americans were so rude. They tended to sever all communication once he'd sent the first reasonably true face pic. Europeans, he'd found, might cringe at the reveal, but could often muster shocked shreds of courtesy – even as they declined his favors. Not like Americans, or at least the ones encountered in his low venue, who sneered, stormed off or occasionally looked inclined to hit him after he opened his apartment door to reveal the medusa behind the dated photos he trafficked. He tried using newer pictures, but they just didn't work as well.

He was the Dorian Gray of yearning internet ads. His true form grew old and corrupted, yet his pictures online remained young and beautiful.

"Eastern European," the ad had said. So it was disappointing when the hustler greeted him with the distinct nasal twang of South Jersey. A little femmy, too. But wasn't that always the way? These magnificent young gods who open their mouths to shriek as shrill 12-year-old girls. What was the line from that Woody Allen movie? "Don't speak!"

Quibbles aside, the hustler was acceptably handsome: Shaved head, tanned, blond features. No twink here, this was a man. He had the build of a b-level action movie star. What had the ad said? Mid 30s, 8.5, fun euro stud. Ready for action.

He took the hustler's coat and delivered a glass of water. As they chatted, he assessed the threat level of this encounter. The hustler smiled when, like a genial horse trader, he squeezed the man's biceps, groped his pecs. The eye contact was friendly, flirty. So different from the resignation of the occasional fly who stuck in his web, too far gone inside his own lust to turn back.

The stack of $20 bills had been in plain view on his dresser. The hustler put down his water and waited expectantly. There was no tingling warning from his spider sense. All systems go. Open the door to your mystery date.

As they sat on the edge of his bed and removed their shoes, he continued his profiling. Manicured eyebrows, bronzer, barbed-wire bicep tattoo. This was no continental gentleman, this was a Chelsea muscle queen. Possibly HIV positive, although that wouldn't matter under his intractable game rules.

I won't suck his dick, he decided. It was the ass that had caught his eye, anyway. Two muscular globes to be gently pulled apart. A rose bud waiting to express its nectar under his probing tongue.

Later, as they rested in a sweaty and sticky knot, he asked the hustler about himself. Since this was the first time he'd bought a full-on hooker – no pretense of massage here – he might as well satisfy his curiosity. It was his time, after all.

The hustler was a cheerful, chatty sort. He said he was just back from working a summer at Fire Island, where he had been a "supplier" at ground zero for gay boys and men, The Pines.

He must have raised a dubious eyebrow, because the hustler quickly clarified that he had worked for one of the dockside bars coordinating incoming shipments from the mainland on the Sayville ferry.

If he'd been a Chelsea queen himself, he might have copped a sassy black girl attitude and said "Uh huh? And what else were you supplying?"

But he let that pass.

Once started, the hustler seemed determined to assert his legitimacy. Perhaps the hustler wanted to run down the clock after the vigorous rogering he had just endured. He had delivered a superb ass-eating, butt-fucking performance. It had seemed important to be in control of the situation.

The chatty hustler who was a "supplier" told of a morning he had gone to The Pines docks to greet the 7:30 a.m. ferry. He described the scene like the aftermath of a suicide bombing. Bodies everywhere, passed-out party boys sprawled on the benches and wooden planks of the tiny harbor. He had gone to the bar where he worked to get a dolly. On the veranda he found five or six tweaked-out, naked men fucking each other bareback.

All this on a Monday morning after one of the biggest parties of the summer, ironically named "Ascension."

The hustler, who was presenting himself as anti-drugs, described the scene as one of the lower circles of hell.

But was it?

It seemed to him, as he rested in a sweaty tangle of limbs, that these men had achieved exactly what they wanted. They had hoarded their money and sexual energy to have a peak experience on vacation at one of the gayest places in the world. They had realized their goal, however destroyed or debased they might seem to someone else.

Wasn't that his own process, without the excessive behavior? He had traversed from legitimate massage to massage with happy ending to, today, full-on prostitute.

If what he wanted was physical contact, why keep battering himself in an arena where his personal currency was diminished? What was the difference, really, between anonymous sex with strangers and anonymous sex with prostitutes? A fine gradation between voluntary action and paid service. No one was keeping score.

His whole journey, it seemed to him, was about clarifying what he wanted from life. As opposed to what he felt was expected of him. When he was young, the pressure to marry had been unrelenting from his parents, his mother. But he had skirted that trap. During all those middle years in the closet, he had made himself a cypher; presenting an impenetrable ambiguity to the world while furtively cruising.

Nothing better than sex when you think you have to sneak it. Uh huh!

But even that questionable facade had dissolved with the years. He was no more or less than a middle-aged gay man whose path had not lead to a shared co-op on the Upper West Side, twin Jack Russell terriers or an Asian baby.

But he still had his faithful kinsman, Lust.

If he could no longer attract beauty, why not buy it? It was logical and easy, if one removed false shame and societal mores from the equation.

It was just a matter of controlling the circumstances to not be sordid.

It was a relief, really, from the joyless vista of rejection and sexlessness. With such a small thing as money, he could keep his fires burning; extend his potency and horndogginess. Perhaps right up to the end, adjusting for age and infirmity.

What would his earnest 20-year-old-self think of this picture, a dirty old man gleefully pawing the go-go boys?

It seemed a tidy solution. He would be like a Greek mentor of old, sharing his experience and resources with beautiful young men. There would always be plenty of them to choose from in Manhattan.

But he had to allow for the possibility that he had missed something glaringly important to other people. A need for intimacy, the comfort of a long-term companion. And now, so far down this solitary road, so deeply enmeshed in hedonism, he could no longer see it anymore.

The hustler stirred and looked at the alarm clock at his bedside. By his calculation they had a good $35 to go. But maybe it didn't work that way. One fuck was all you got.

What do you want to do, asked the hustler.

I don't know, he said.

Did you cum?

No.

A moment passed in silence as he noted the deepening shadows in his room. It was that time of the afternoon when the light starts to go faster.

Then, said the hustler, rolling onto his stomach, I think you should fuck me again.

So he did.

The Prodigal Prince

"My son."

The queen, his mother, swept into the receiving room in a rustle of black and gold finery. With a well-practiced flourish, she held out her knuckles for him to kneel and kiss in the courtly manner. Still fuming over his rough summons to court, he did not. After a moment she took back her hand and turned away from him until the serving ladies retired.

"Your manners have grown coarse in these years away. It is ill-done to shame a queen before her servants."

She looked tired. And older than he remembered. Though still beautiful, there was a looseness to her skin he'd never seen before. Shocking tributaries of silver threatened to swamp her auburn luster. That was her pride, he knew, of all her charms — her crown of thick red hair.

She in turn was regarding him: His stringy flaxen mane, longer than the fashion; and the blue eyes, his father's eyes, cornflower blue. Thin, flat-chested and altogether too small for his years. He could see her critiquing him as the product of her body; noting how the last five years had changed him. And judging how best to bend him to her will.

Tired, yes. And thin. But still churning with the irrepressible energy of her ambitions.

What was she up to, this warrior in women's robes? What was she plotting, this schemer? Was it as Jonathan said? Was he to be married off to some minor princess?

His breath quickened and grew shallow as he envisioned himself at the great altar, trapped in a marriage ceremony to some strange girl. He was seized by a familiar demon, the impulse to take to his heels and flee.

I am not a boy anymore, he told himself. I am a grown man of 25 years. I will marry or not as I choose, queen be damned! Only I must be careful, for she is full of guile and manipulations.

He picked up a steaming mug of mulled wine and turned to look out one of the long vertical windows in the palace receiving room. The sun was setting and his view of the castle walls and the great city outside was obscured by a burst of orange light. Bedazzled by the glare, he closed his eyes and accepted the sun's pale heat on his grimy face.

It had been this same time, a fading afternoon three days ago, when the guards came for him...

As the son of a king, Galan had grown up in a glare of scrutiny shining back to his earliest memories. The most mundane transactions of his boyhood in Hyperia Court were followed by adult eyes watching, gauging, calculating. His first steps, fevers and hunts became fodder for court gossip. Jovial men slapped him on the back after Galan's first kill. Court bawds winked slyly on the day his manly emissions first presented in the royal bedclothes. Ambitious ladies pushed their sons, and later their daughters, to befriend the young prince.

Some children might thrive in the bright sun of such constant attention. But Galan was a shy lad, ill-suited to endure the unblinking gaze of royal watchers. Much of his childhood had been spent acquiring a shell to help him perform, as an awkward actor might, his ill-cast role.

Fortunately, Galan's shortcomings hadn't been a major trouble for the kingdom; for he was the third son. It didn't matter so much that Prince Galan, the odd one, had hid from his birthday hunt; or vomited, sometimes, during the family's ceremonial appearances.

When the other flaw was revealed, King Arnow wasted no time in dispatching his youngest son to Pinetop, the summer palace in the northern foothills. Calling Pinetop a palace was heavy gilding for the crude, sprawling farmhouse and stables; but it had long been a place of refuge and rest for the royal family. Galan had grown to lonely manhood as lord of the empty country estate.

Until the chilly evening three days past, when the king's guards thundered into the courtyard at Pinetop, scattering chickens in their wake. The sergeant of the guard, Galan remembered him, Conor was his name, had slid off his heaving horse and thrust into Galan's hand an urgent summons to court from Queen Magritte. Galan had barely read down to his mother's florid signature when Conor barked out what could only be described as orders to the young prince: They would leave at dawn, riding fresh horses from the garrison down the road.

And here he was now, thinking his thoughts while the queen of the realm waited upon him. The sun had dropped in the sky; Galan could now see the lights in the windows and plumes of smoke from the many chimneys outside the castle wall. He roused himself from his reverie and girded himself to face his mother.

But Magritte would answer no questions. She

bade him dine with her in her private chambers after he'd washed off the dust of his journey. The queen hustled out of the room, not waiting for him to snub her again.

A footman led Galan to one of the guest chambers near the main hall. As they walked through the corridors, servants nodded and maids curtsied to the young prince. Strange to be treated with such studied courtesy. He'd discouraged it to the country folk at Pinetop.

It was eight winters since he'd left Hyperia Court; at 17 years, in disgrace. His last return had been at 20, a debacle.

A boisterous fire crackled and pulsed in the guest quarters, one of a half-dozen airy rooms used for court visitors of high station. Above the mantel hung a large scarlet tapestry with the royal emblem finely stitched in threads of gold and brown and black. The mountain lion in profile; pointed ear, a single red eye, and a narrow tail curving beneath it like a coat hook.

The hearth flames darted about a black cauldron hanging from a stout swinging yardarm. A portly manservant of middle years supervised the transfer of steaming buckets of water from the cauldron into a finely crafted wooden tub with large wheels on one end, in the fashion of a gardener's wheelbarrow. Assisting in the task were two boys struggling to not slop their buckets.

Forcing himself to the expected role, Galan disrobed and stepped into the tub. He suffered himself to be bathed, his hair pulled free of twigs and tangles. The steaming water soothed his sore muscles from the hard ride.

On the other side of the cheery room, a pair

of black breeches and a dark green shirt were laid out on the large pallet. He wouldn't need the shabby clothes that Jonathan had hunted up for the journey.

"She's going to marry you off, you know."

That's what Jonathan had said, that night at Pinetop as Galan packed for the journey to court. He'd stood in the doorway of their bedroom, one hand holding an oft-mended white tunic he'd rustled up. His other hand grasped a pair of gleaming knee-high boots bearing the obvious polish of the garrison.

"I knew it couldn't last forever, my lord. I often told you so. Princes must marry princesses," Jonathan said with a half-sad, half-satisfied smile.

"'Tis a sudden thing ... and worrisome," said Galan. "It would be good to have a friend at court."

It took some beseeching from Galan, playing on Jonathan's lifelong wish to see the great city. But the next morning Jonathan was waiting with him in the courtyard in the icy pre-dawn. Jonathan held the reins of his father's gray mare. They waited in the dark until the four guards rode in leading a fifth, rider-less horse.

But Conor would have none of their plan to bring Jonathan along. Galan remembered him better now, the arrogant way the sergeant had shepherded Galan's initial ouster from court, barely acknowledging the disgraced prince.

When Galan protested, Conor ordered the other guards to hoist Galan upon his saddle and bind his wrists to the pommel. They galloped out of the courtyard, sending Jonathan's nag running off on its own.

Sitting in the tub, Galan rubbed his wrists where the leather cords had bound him. There were no marks, for he had quickly been cut free once the journey was underway. No physical marks; just the indignity of being trussed like a chicken going to market, fuss though he might. He'd forgotten that, the tyranny of Hyperia Court, where the king's will was absolute and unbending.

Jonathan. Always looking out for Galan, helping him deal with the homesteaders at Pinetop, the servants and farmers. Would he ever see Jonathan again? Or was that all over? Fine, manly Jonathan with his strong nose, black curls and easy smile. Jonathan had the look of a true king's son, not the sunken-chested ghost at his side. Standing with Jonathan in the dusty parlor room at Pinetop, looking at their naked selves in the cloudy mirror over the mantel.

The queen made small talk during their dinner of roasted pheasant, grilled onions and squash. How familiar were these rooms to him! The sitting room where they now dined, with discreet hallways leading away on either side. How often had the little princes played on that same striped rug before the hearth.

Magritte had dressed for dinner in the scarlet and gold of the realm. She had painted her face for him. She kept their wine goblets filled and turned away inquiries after his father and brothers. At times she treated Galan as if he were some foreign courtier for her to charm. Other times she spoke as a mother might, chiding him for the length of his hair, his thinness.

He remembered her scolding him as a child after his behavior had marred some function or another. The ceremonial duties of a royal family weighed upon Galan, who suffered from intense moments of panic during public outings. How often she had stressed that appearances must be kept up, that he, they, didn't have the luxury of being weak.

"Don't worry about your servant, my son," Magritte said during the meal. "It was silly to think you would need a manservant from the country here."

Galan kept his eyes on his plate and made no reply.

After the servants cleared the table, she led Galan to two padded footstools by the hearth. They drank their wine in silence and the mood grew somber. Galan waited. Finally Magritte reached into a hidden pocket in her dress and then held out her hand.

On her palm were two rings. The heavy gold signet of King Arnow and a ruby solitaire favored by his brother Jacques.

"I found these in a drawer of my table," she said, her eyes motioning to her dressing table littered with small boxes and vials of unguents. Galan could remember hanging on to the table's spindly legs and watching his mother apply her womanly wiles in an imported mirror of famed clarity. How beautiful she was, still.

Galan picked up his father's ring. It was heavy in his hand, a great tabletop of a ring. On its square surface was the raised profile of a mountain lion, with a tiny ruby eye. Same as the tapestry, the Hyperian lion, king of the mountains.

"Where are they," he asked.

"Your father and Jacques left with ten men to settle some claims in the east. A fortnight ago."

Much of King Arnow's authority came from making regular visits to the far corners of his kingdom. Grievances among the townsfolk waited to be settled at the king's roving tribunals. And if taxes were collected at the same time, few found the courage to complain to the king directly. It was not unusual for the king, and in recent years, Jacques, to be gone a month or more on their trips. He started to say as much to his mother, as if comforting a fretful old woman. But what was the meaning of the rings?

"Are they ... ransomed?"

"They're dead, my son."

He stared at her, finally shaking his head, no.

"They're dead, Galan. Your father and brother are murdered."

"How can you know?"

She pointed at her dressing table. Her hand shook and for the first time she seemed to lose a little of her famed composure.

"Someone came in here, my most private chamber, and left this most foul evidence of their evil deed. To ... taunt me, to weaken my resolve."

She stood up angrily and walked over to her dressing table. She brought back a small wooden box and lifted the lid. Inside were four locks of hair, each tied with a different-colored snippet of ribbon. She lifted two of the locks of hair and held them in her fingers.

"Some of what they say is true," Magritte said. "Not that I needed trickery to hold your father's eye. But yes, my mother. My mother was a woman of power."

With her free hand, Magritte reached inside her bodice and pulled forth a narrow finger of rose quartz mounted on a slender chain. Few knew she wore such a humble stone, hidden amid her pendants and chains. When he was a child, his grandmother had shown him the intricate carvings on the metal mount for the polished quartz. She'd said it was a relic of The Hyperians, the invaders who conquered them so many generations ago.

"My mother taught me some of her art. A little."

She held the quartz in her thumb and forefinger, gazing into its milky pinkness. Then she shook the two locks of hair in Galan's direction.

"With these I can know. For those I love. Be they well, be they ill."

She restored the stone to its fleshy berth and put the two locks of hair gently back into the box.

Galan watched the fading firelight flicker across his mother's back. He was still holding his father's ring.

"Where's Phillip?"

Magritte got up and led Galan down the hall to the servant's alcove. Behind the curtain, his brother was laid out on a narrow bed. Elise, the queen's most trusted lady, sat at bedside squeezing drops of broth from a rag into Phillip's mouth. His teeth were clenched and his skin was gray.

"He fell ill the same day I found the rings. He became weaker, until this ..."

They watched as Elise tried to guide the corner of rag into Phillip's lips, like a wet nurse's teat. When she squeezed, the soup ran down the side of his unmoving face.

They left Phillip. Magritte walked Galan to the door of her chamber.

"We must be careful what we eat and drink," she said. She seemed suddenly to be teetering with exhaustion. The weariness from his trip, along with the shock of the news, was taking its toll on Galan as well.

Galan knew, even before he tried, that she would not take back the royal signet. He buried it in his pocket before heading down the hall.

In later years, King Galan would try to reweave in his mind the night his path to the throne unexpectedly cleared. He could never make whole cloth of it, only scraps. He could see his mother's scarlet dress, the gold thread on her ample bosom; but not her face. He could feel the heft of his father's ring, screaming its presence in his hip pocket as he lurched through the corridors outside his mother's chamber. He remembered shaking off a servant who mistook shock and exhaustion for too much wine; the tiny mocking smile on the servant's face that erased itself under Galan's stare. The sleepy boys relieving him of his boots and garments in the dim light from the embers. He'd ordered them to leave him, after they'd put him to bed. But they'd stayed, huddled together on their mat by the hearth. Even the servant boys defied him.

That was closer to it, the true thing that Galan could rekindle in his mind. The servant's mocking smile, the cowering boys disobeying him. The sergeant in the courtyard barking out orders to the prince; his mother's orders. Being tied to the saddle like some wench won in battle. That, too, would have come only from the queen. Even the order to stop Jonathan. That was Magritte. Magritte knew all of it. It was foolish to think he had any secrets, even at his country farm up north. He was the son of the king, all eyes were watching ... He was the king.

Rage turning to dread in an instant, like a

sweaty summer leap into an icy mountain lake. His father was dead. Jacques was dead. Galan had no doubt of his mother's certainty. She would know, in the way she knew many things. His father and brother murdered; and Phillip dying. They were under attack; and he, Galan, the odd prince, was a laughable hero to win the day in this tale.

He had hidden the ring in his fist as the boys undressed him. He held it clenched to his chest as sleep finally washed away his roiling thoughts.

In the morning, Galan took advantage of a momentary absence by the boys to stuff the ring deep into the lining of his pallet. When he lay back he could feel it, somewhat, a hard lump in the dense clumps of goat hair; but it would have to do. He dressed himself in new finery set out by the boys and headed to the main hall.

In the absence of King Arnow, Queen Magritte was presiding over an audience with couriers and townspeople. All eyes turned to Galan, as he stepped through the curtains and joined a huddle of court advisors at the right of the dual thrones. He had thought, in his usual awkward way, to watch from the wings. But of course that wouldn't do. Magritte frowned for an instant and then corrected herself.

"The court welcomes our most beloved son."

She gestured for him to join her on the dais. Galan reluctantly came forward.

"I think the king, your father, would not mind if his son rested from his journey."

Magritte nodded to the throne beside her, the larger of two elaborately-carved oak chairs. Galan smoothed his face into a neutral mask and joined her amid a surprised buzz from the assemblage. Anyone who knew King Arnow knew that he *would* mind someone sitting on his throne, even one of his sons.

Galan settled beside the queen, who returned her attention to a dispute between two traders. Galan held his face immobile as he tried to steady his breath. Of all the breathless, panicky moments he'd known as a child, to preside over an audience seated in the king's throne was a new threshold of fear. He felt sweaty and lightheaded. Fortunately, as an outsider he was not expected to weigh in.

As the applicants to the court came and went, his nerves steadied. Galan was able to relax his fixed demeanor and study the court. There were at least 50 people in the chamber, and dozens more coming and going in the adjoining main hallway. He had forgotten what a busy place was Hyperia Court.

To his right were the advisors: Fat Humphris, Box the groveler and a few others he vaguely recognized. To his left, past Magritte, were two courtiers who wore the green and gray of Auberlain, the much larger kingdom to the north and east of Hyperia. Beyond them was Jacques' wife Catherine. And behind her, just coming into view, was her brother René.

René; vile, evil René. Erratic, cruel René, who had pursued Galan so ruthlessly during the fortnight of Jacques and Catherine's wedding five years ago. Pursued Galan like the most ardent swain, only to laugh about it with his friends after he'd won his wager that he could steal a kiss from the king's son. Nothing in private, never anything in private. Always someone watching, telling tales, seeking advantage. It had been the final humiliation that sent Galan up north for good.

René, even more devilishly handsome than

ever, with his pointed chin and wicked brown eyes, winking even now at Galan up on the throne.

It was more than one could stand; and it would be his life from now on.

At the end of the audience, René took his sister's arm, keeping his hand on her elbow as they left the hall. His manner struck Galan as something other than brotherly, more like one protecting a prized possession.

They took a late lunch in Magritte's chambers – fruits and vegetables they could prepare themselves, dried meats and cheeses culled from the kitchen solely by Elise.

In the light of day, and after the normal business of the court, his mother's revelations seemed like a sinister communication from a dream realm; a troubling vision to be cast off in the sun. It was all a misunderstanding; the king and Jacques would return soon. Perhaps Magritte bespelled herself, as well. Both seemed determined to put aside the shadow of their loss, if only for an hour.

Galan watched as his mother pushed her finely embroidered dress sleeves past her elbows and began chopping potatoes and onions to fry in the pig grease. An hour ago she had presided over a room full of the rich and powerful. Now she was aproned and wielding a broad knife like any scullery girl. Seeing something in her son's gaze, she smiled and brushed a strand of hair out of her face.

"Well I wasn't always a queen," she said wryly, arching one eyebrow.

As he washed some green trout to fry up with the potatoes, Galan thought about his mother, trying to see her as others might. Who was she, really? A witch from the South who'd stolen the king's favor –

a notorious scandal. And her mother, a wrinkled old terror who would box the ears of any court lady who put on airs to her.

Grandmother Rose had told the boys she and Magritte hailed from a magical floating island in the sea of Margray. It had been a disappointment that summer, when the royal family made the trip by boat to visit the queen's clan on Pedregon. The magical island had been filled with fishermen and goatherds. Galan, young as he was at the time, had sensed his mother's shame before the king at her rustic background. His father had been his usual glacial self, neither rude nor especially cordial to her kinsfolk.

Why did she care so much about this court, this foreign land? Always so formal, what were her feelings for Arnow, her sons? She'd done nothing to intervene, at least that Galan had seen, when at 17 he was sent from court in disgrace after a fumbling dalliance with a stable boy. The king became enraged at the report of his son being buggered in the straw. King Arnow had barely looked at Galan after he'd learned of it.

The queen might have spoken up, argued that a little play between youths was not unheard of, was possibly normal. The companionship of farm lads on a cold winter's night. And such things were not just for youths. Galan had heard of the military camps, how a man could be a warrior and yet also a "soldier's friend," as it was known.

No, the shame had been that a king's son, one who could have his pick of any lady in the court, would prefer the crude substitute of a man. One did such things when conditions dictated, but never from choice. Or was it that Galan had played the girl in the romp? Jonathan and he switched roles like a swordsman's feint, the blade passing from hand to hand. And neither the less for it.

Jonathan. Was he missing Galan as much as he did him?

"He came to court at mid-spring," said Magritte when the conversation turned to René and the omnipresent delegation from Auberlain.

"Your sister," she said with a wisp of disdain, "Felt lonely and sent for her dear brother. Who has little to occupy himself at home, too far from his own throne to matter."

Jonathan. They'd never had a chance to say goodbye, after their rough parting. What would Jonathan do now? Surely he would marry now, and take over his father's farm. Galan had sometimes wondered whether his novelty as a king's son had wrongly lured Jonathan off his true path. He would be better off now, freed of this perverse glamour.

But to never have said goodbye, and told him what a fine fellow he was and what a difference it had meant to Galan to know him.

"What ails you, prince," said his mother.

Heart pounding, Galan almost spoke up. But what would his words be?

"Nothing ... I just ... I suspect this brother ... his presence."

She eyed him a moment, arching one eyebrow.

"Well, better late than never, my lord. You do well to be cautious. But rest assured, that envoy of Auberlain is well-watched."

Galan's face colored with shame. Another of Magritte's double-edged thrusts. His mother knew everything, she made that her business.

They dined in silence until Magritte gasped. Cutting into the side of her trout, she'd found a long white worm burrowed through the length of the poor fish's side. She stared at it, her face going white.

"'Tis but a worm, mother," Galan said, as he took her plate and dumped the trout in a slop bucket. He served her another from the skillet, but Magritte would eat no more.

Magritte's attempt to buy time was abruptly ended at mid-week. Emissaries from Auberlain arrived from the eastern border with alarming news of an ambush at the royal camp. The king, prince and entire royal party slain by robbers, their belongings ransacked. The bodies arrived two days later. The court was thrown into a frenzy the likes of which it had never seen, preparing for the burial of the king and his oldest son.

After several hours of prayers and laments, Magritte, Galan and Catherine – with René close at hand – led a procession outside the castle walls. A great pyre was lit in the north field. Plumes of perfumed white smoke swirled in the wind, blowing this way and that. The bodies of royalty were always burned to thwart trophy hunters. There were contradictory traditions involving the royals. It was dangerous, if not fatal, for he who spilled royal blood. But it was good luck to have a tooth or lock of royal hair. King Arnow had kept a tooth off his father, King Laurent. Galan had seen it, embedded in a gold lump his father sometimes wore on a chain.

It was bitterly cold. The trees had lost all their leaves although the snow had been late to come this year. As the funeral oils burned away, the pyre gave off a more acrid smoke. After getting a smoky blast full-on, Galan coughed and blinked his smarting eyes. He found himself looking at a man across the heat-rippled air. A countryman in traveling clothes, shaggy and long-bearded. He stared at Galan directly, so different from the bowing and covert looks from the servants and courtiers. Galan found himself unable to turn away from the man's eyes.

It came to him, as if the man were standing by his side and whispering in his ear: *"I would speak with you."*

It was popular lore that the royals had rare abilities, a tradition encouraged and played upon by the family. Most of the great battle stories of their past kings had some magical component, whether real or embellished. And, of course, the Hyperians had been known for their dark arts and advanced weaponry, which they used to conquer and rule this land before disappearing suddenly from history.

In his speeches, King Arnow invoked dreams to impress his will upon the court. Galan remembered watching his father summon a salt shaker to slide shakily across the table to his hand as visiting envoys watched in shocked silence. Years later, Phillip had told him that it was a ruse; that Jacques had been underneath the table pulling the shaker along with a needle stuck up between the planks.

As boys, the princes had tried with little success to speak to each other without words; or move floating leaves without touching them. Jacques was popular with the ladies, and Phillip had a way with the beasts; but those were hardly magical powers.

If anyone had true magic, it was the

111

interlopers onto the royal lineage: The witches of Pedregon. Flamboyant Grandma Rose, who took to court finery with the garish enthusiasm of a goatherd's daughter; wrapping colored scarves around her head and reading futures in the lines of an upturned hand. And rightly, more often than not.

And beautiful Magritte, who always seemed to know what one was thinking; or when lies were told or plots hatched. Magritte had known when Rose died. Galan had watched the tears sliding down her cheeks, and cried a little himself. They'd been away at Pinetop; their hastily-assembled caravan had met the messengers mid-way on the road back to court.

When he was 11, Galan fell dangerously ill with a bone fever that had claimed many children and elderly at court. At a low point, he had dreamed his mother's white cat was running ahead of him in the twilight. A glimmering white form urging him through the dark woods, even as he longed to stop and rest. But that had been only a dream.

As the pyre reached its peak, Catherine fainted, landing face down in the hard-packed turf. In the tumult to get her back to the castle, Galan slipped away. He pulled his plain cloak tight about his court finery and kept his eyes lowered. When he wasn't standing next to his mother or riding with court guards, there were few who would recognize him. The young prince gone so long.

He sought out the stranger. By silent assent they walked together into the bustling streets of Hyperia.

"Will you have a pint with me," the man asked. Galan nodded.

They said no more until they were seated in a roadhouse in a workmen's section of Hyperia unfamiliar to Galan. There'd been a wooden carving swinging above the door with the antlered heads of two crudely-rendered beasts: The Two Stags.

A hairy, heavily-rouged barmaid brought them two tankards. After taking a long drink of ale, the man regarded Galan with his strange eyes. When he spoke, his tone was light, almost mocking.

"'Tis a sad day. And an unexpected turn for the young prince."

The man's manner of speech reminded Galan of the envoys and court advisers who used words the way soldiers wielded swords. If the stranger expected Galan to respond in kind he had chosen the wrong royal, for of course Galan had no head for such games. He was simple and direct when about the hunt.

"I heard you ... in my mind."

"Did you now," said the man, taking another pull on his tankard. When he set it down, his grizzled mustache was white with spume. His hair was long and unruly, his brown beard going to gray. His clothes were dusty and stained, as if he had just arrived on one of the many roads that lead to Hyperia Court.

"Are you royal," asked Galan.

The man looked at Galan a long time, sizing him up. Behind the mocking pose, there was something guarded in his eyes; hurts and long resentments and more that Galan couldn't read. Galan became uneasy looking into those eyes. He turned away and looked across the crowded roadhouse. So many men shouting and arguing, an undercurrent of excitement in the air. It wasn't every day they buried a king. Although they seemed to be enjoying themselves a tad too much for such a somber occasion.

"I'm the king's own brother. I am your Uncle William."

Galan's eyes snapped back to the stranger. William? William had died a long time ago, before Galan was born.

"The prince died. The man did not."

The stranger waved for two more tankards. As they drank, he told a tale of growing up in Hyperia Court with Arnow as the older brother and heir apparent. There had been a sister between them who died young. He spoke with so many details of life at court and Pinetop, and with such insight into Arnow's nature, that Galan soon believed that this man was, indeed, his Uncle William.

And they were linked by more than blood. It became clear that his uncle shared the same queer nature as Galan, and had met the same downfall. William's tale echoed Galan's experience: A scandal with the young son of a powerful merchant; a banishment. Only in William's story it was permanent exile from the kingdom, under a ruse that the king's brother had died from fever.

"If not for your mother, I think he would have had me done off, like an idiot child or a bag of kittens. His own brother," said William, as a look of utter bitterness crossed his creased face.

"My mother?"

"Aye. She spoke up for me. It was her idea for me to slip away."

Galan was well-soused as he made his unsteady way back to the castle. His brain was reeling from his strange parting from the uncanny uncle. He set his swirling thoughts aside as he navigated home. The streets were filled with torches and bonfires, people toasting the old king and cursing the Auberlain dogs. There was excitement in the air, a sense of change and uncertainty. This is history, thought Galan, the likes of which you don't see hidden away in the countryside.

He skirted a crowd where a young firebrand was making a call to war in the name of Arnow. He could picture that: King Arnow and Prince Jacques leading the troops in battle. Galan tried to summon up sorrow in his heart for them, but could find little. His father had been cold and disapproving; his brother indifferent. Phillip. Phillip had been kinder.

Such a strange day: The funeral, the man across the pyre. And here's the prince, the king, weaving through the dark streets like any village wastrel. It was odd to see the lights of the castle towering ahead, and feel so apart from them. It occurred to Galan that he could fail to return. Disappear, as in William's strange tale. Go live on a farm with Jonathan, the two of them.

It felt as if a great door was opening in Galan's mind, the idea that he could step off the royal path he had walked since his earliest memories. It had never occurred to him that he could be something other than a king's son.

I'm free, he thought to himself. In this moment, I am free to do whatever I want.

As Galan neared the gates to the castle, a figure darted out from the shadows, grabbing Galan's arm and pulling him into a dark alley.

"Galan! Is that you? Oh praise be!"

It was Jonathan! Without a thought of what any might think, Galan pulled Jonathan into a hug of bruising closeness. Jonathan was shivering in the cold night air. Galan wrapped his cloak around him.

Whispering in the shadows, they exchanged tales. Jonathan, alarmed at the forceful way the guards had taken Galan, had determined to follow once he'd caught the gray mare. But soldiers from the garrison had stopped him on the road, and taken him to one of the holding rooms at the fort. They'd kept him there a week, never saying why. He'd finally escaped after one of his young cousins slipped past a slumbering guard and freed him.

Fearful of returning to the palace at Pinetop or his father's farm, he'd taken directly to the main road; hiding in the brush when the garrison guards came looking. He'd caught a ride on a trader's wagon and then spent the past few days lurking outside the castle, watching for Galan to leave, fearful of being detained anew. He looked the worse for his travails, thin and dirty.

"We never said goodbye," Jonathan said.

Galan in turn told his sad story, the deaths, Phillip's illness.

"Why ... then you'll be king," said Jonathan, wonderingly.

Jonathan swayed on his feet, near collapse. Galan put his arm around his waist and started to walk Jonathan to the castle. But he stopped before stepping out of the shadows. The servants, the court people, Magritte, René. Jonathan, his companion, his true love. They would know, everyone would know. Talking, whispering, laughing. He ... couldn't.

Galan's hand fell onto the small coin pouch at his belt. It came to him. He would hide Jonathan away at the roadhouse. He started to tell Jonathan about his meeting with the odd uncle, but stopped. It was too strange, too shameful. He had to think further about William. He slipped the purse into Jonathan's hand and unfastened his cloak.

"I may not be able to come right away. It's not safe, and I ... I don't want them to find you, to know about you. Just not yet, you understand?"

Jonathan nodded. With a dispirited gait he wobbled down the street towards the Two Stags.

Shivering without his cloak, Galan hurried towards the castle gates. The guards had evidently been told not to make a fuss, for they let Galan pass with little fanfare. He didn't need the fabled royal powers to know that Magritte would be waiting for him in his quarters.

She was sitting by the hearth, warming her bare feet at the fire. Her fur-lined cloak was spread across the back of her chair, and she was dressed in a loose dressing gown. No servant boys. She looked as if she'd been waiting a long time; drinking, simmering. Her eyes met his with steely coolness.

The little table was laid with cold meats, cheese and pears. His eyes must have lit up at the spread, for she gestured for him to sit down. He did so, pouring himself some wine and refilling her mug.

"I had forgotten my lord's fear of ... the public spectacle. I thought he would have grown out of it, as he might leave many boyish things behind."

She took a sip and continued speaking coolly, as if trying to see both sides of the coin.

"But I suppose life at court is strange and fearsome for one who has lived quietly in the country," she said with a disappointed sigh.

Galan's mouth was stuffed with cold fowl. Whether it be from the ale or just that he was a man now, he found he wasn't afraid of his mother's gibes. He took a long time to finish chewing and then a big swig of wine, surprising himself with his coolness at making her wait. When he finally answered her, he found unexpected strength in speaking honestly.

"I spied someone in the crowd and determined to have a chat with him. We went off and had a tankard. Several."

"I know who you saw," she snapped, dropping all pretense of equanimity. "Do you think I don't have eyes in my head, or nose to smell a foul beast when it comes scratching?"

"Is it true? What he said? That you saved him from my father?"

"It was my mother's plan! We wanted him out of court! And no royal blood spilled by your father's hand. Mark me, have nothing more to do with that one. He is canny like a fox, and beguiling like a snake. He bears no goodwill for any of us."

Galan shrugged.

"It was pleasant to have an audience with ... kin ... without having to be bound and dragged upon a horse."

Magritte slammed her mug down, slopping wine onto the table.

"Listen you fool. Do you think I'm here to scold the little prince for running off? Much has transpired in these hours, while my lord was out swilling. ... And if he would be king one day, he would mark me well!"

She had his attention now, and he waited for her to compose herself. When she spoke again, it was in cooler tones.

"Our Catherine claims to be with child, your brother's child."

A surge of pure relief flowed through Galan. A child, Jacques's child! Magritte could be regent. She would love that, it was her destiny. He would go back north and be with Jonathan.

His mother stared at him, plainly disgusted by the joy washing across him. When he spoke, he dropped his taunting manner and tried to speak as before, honestly.

"Would that be so bad ... mother? You were born to rule, while I ..."

He shrugged; a small lift of the shoulders that carried a lifetime of ineptitude.

She looked at him sadly.

"A kingdom needs a king, my son. A babe on the throne invites trouble, like a lone chick in an unguarded henhouse."

After a moment, she put her hand to her bosom and spoke imperiously, as if recounting a family history to an assemblage.

"A long time ago, your grandmother –"

She stopped herself, as if thinking better of it. She continued in a different vein.

"Your brother was not a good husband to our poor Catherine. He bored with her quickly, I'm afraid. ... As you know, from his earliest days he was well-versed in the wenches at court."

She took a long sip of wine and then looked about on the floor for her house slippers, digging into them with her toes.

"In all these years of harlotry, there have been no bastards. No creditable ones," she said.

"Virgin upon virgin, and none took spark. Your brother's affliction seems to have been a serious one for us, for the royal line."

As everyone at court knew, Jacques had but one egg. Galan had heard jokes about it growing up. But they'd generally been mild ones, reflecting admiration for the young prince's robustness and appetite. One egg good enough for two men. A royal egg to do the work of two.

Moving heavily, Magritte rose to her feet. She wrapped herself in her cloak and walked unsteadily past him. At the door, she turned for a parting shot, again the steely-eyed queen staring down an opponent. She put her hand to her bosom, and Galan knew she was grasping the rose quartz through her robe.

"She bears no fruit from our tree."

After settling into bed, Galan's head whirled with images of the funeral: His father, Jacques, Jonathan, Catherine, René, Magritte.

But as he slipped off to sleep it was William, his uncanny uncle, who appeared to him. William leaning forward to him on the roadhouse bench, placing his hand high on Galan's thigh.

"I have my room up above," said William, his eyes shining strangely. "Will ye come up lad? I have a hankering for a taste of royal milk."

The next day, Magritte hosted a late supper in her chambers for René and Catherine. Magritte stocked the table with roasted chicken, leg of lamb, sweet ears of corn and spicy stewed pumpkin. It was an awkward meal. Galan was suffering the effects of last night's grog; as he suspected was also true for the queen.

"It is good to see your majesty up and about. When he left the funeral, his subjects were concerned he might be indisposed, as of old."

René, speaking the stilted talk of the courtier. Full of himself and obviously holding some secret advantage. Was it as his mother said? Was it René's babe that Catherine was carrying? Or did he force another man on her? It was monstrous.

René and Catherine. He so devilish and scheming, she downcast and cowering.

Galan nodded curtly and Magritte took the conversation elsewhere. He watched as she parried with René, easily reading and returning each implied meaning in his flowery words. It occurred to Galan that just as a mother cat teaches her kittens to hunt, Magritte was conducting a class. Trying to include him in the game, enlist him to her cause.

Since his abduction from Pinetop, Galan had carried within his bosom a hard ball of anger towards his mother, glowing in his heart like the blacksmith's molten metal. His anger found quick tinder in the years of rejection by the family. His exile had been complete: No visits, no letters. Were she still living, his grandmother Rose would have defied such a ban, king or no. But the others deferred; or didn't care. The years of dismissal had left a rime of bitterness upon Galan's heart.

Yet here she was, of middle age and a widow now, fighting with all her wit for ... for what? For power? Fighting ... defending ... the life she had made for herself in this foreign court. Her tireless spirit moved Galan. She was what she was and did what she did with an inner sureness of her own judgment that was both maddening and admirable. Might as well tell a rooster not to crow. Or the snow not to fall.

As he watched her, the crust of resentment melted away. He resolved to enter the game.

"My mother tells me of our good news," he said, turning to Catherine.

She twitched at being addressed directly by

him. She had a bruise on her cheek from her fall; or had her brother hit her? Galan felt sorry to have frightened her, for she seemed a gentle creature. Catherine hung her head and mumbled thanks.

"My sister's heart is overfull with the long-awaited blessing, even though it comes at such a sad time."

"Pray she be delivered safely," said Magritte with a strange look in her eye.

After they left, Magritte raged over René's insistence that a court audience be held on the morrow to receive the delegation from Auberlain. She had insisted that none could be held during this week of mourning, but he had stood firm. There would be a hearing, whether she attended it or not.

"Even now the court is filling with soldiers from Auberlain," said Magritte.

"But why," said Galan.

She looked at him pityingly.

"Can you not guess? Are the ways of intrigue so foreign that you cannot divine your rival's intent?"

She waited.

"To ... enforce ... some claim on the child," said Galan. Such an effort to think this way, and yet so obvious once glimpsed. He despaired of himself.

"Yes. To declare René regent for his sister's baby. Or some such."

A look of fear and sadness crossed Magritte's face. Galan took hold of her arm to steady her. The moment passed and Magritte was back to strategizing.

"Perhaps you should speak with your poor brother's widow," said Magritte, as if thinking aloud. "Is that the answer? Shall you marry our poor Catherine? She's a sad little mouse. But what matter, if she gives us sons."

The great hall was filled with Hyperia's wealthiest and most powerful citizens. They were joined by a conspicuous delegation of 20 Auberlain sentries and a half-dozen officers, the latter visibly angry at having waited three long days for the audience. After extensive condolences from the envoy, a general clad in ceremonial garb delivered a curt proclamation. King Abner of Auberlain appointed his nephew René de St. Pois as lawful regent in Hyperia Court for his niece Catherine's child.

The sentries parted ranks and from their midst stepped René, decked out in the green and gray colors of an Auberlain noble. He held his head high, as if trying to will length into his small frame. The effect was of a pompous little man trying not to sneer at the peasants.

The court erupted with outrage and the Auberlain sentries tightened their ranks. As one, the Auberlainers and Hyperians turned their eyes from René to the throne where Magritte and Galan sat still as stone.

Magritte waited for the tumult to die down. Was she expecting him to speak? Galan felt himself buffeted by a storm-force need to jump up and flee the court room. A cold sweat broke across his brow and blood hammered in his ears. He gripped the carved hand rests of the throne, anchoring himself.

"Our heart is warmed by this declaration of concern from our dear friend and kinsman," said Magritte. "And we welcome his kind offer to help raise our most beloved grandchild, should it be so."

The general nodded, seeming unsure whether Magritte was accepting his declaration or dancing around it.

"But we must point out that the child, should it be so, also has another uncle in this court."

She inclined her head to him. This was his cue to speak up. So many eyes, all upon him, waiting. A white cloud passed before his eyes and the roaring in his ears grew thunderous. His heart was racing, he was close to fainting; he mustn't!

As the court faded into whiteness, Galan imagined he could hear the bemused voice of his newfound uncle: *"This isn't for you, lad."*

After an unknowable amount of time passed, the whiteness receded and Galan could see the court again. René appeared to have made some jest; there were uncertain smiles from the Hyperian citizens standing near him. Galan tried to swallow, but found sand.

The general, unfazed by Magritte's introduction of a second uncle, began to read King Abner's proclamation again. He drowned out Magritte's attempts to interrupt. As he neared the end of his second reading, the general's manner became more bellicose.

Magritte stood her ground, cool and regal.

"The line of succession in Hyperia will not be dictated to her by Auberlain or anyone else," she said calmly. "My late lord and liege had not passed the crown at the time of his untimely and most suspicious death."

An angry murmur rose from the court, and the Auberlain delegation again tightened ranks, hands upon the hilts of their sheathed swords.

"From my late king, the crown now passes to our second son Phillip, who has been grievously ill but lies recovering in my own chambers."

She stood up to end the audience.

"So you see, your lord's proclamation, however well intended, is ill-timed and baseless. The court rejects it. And now you must take leave of a poor woman's heart and allow her to shed a widow's tears in private."

The general seemed on the verge of reading his proclamation a third time. But Magritte was already sweeping past him out of the chambers. The general gave a curt salute to the departing queen and rejoined his delegation.

The audience was over. The chamber roared with everyone speaking at the same time, giving their take on what had just happened. Some of the court advisors were eyeing Galan dubiously, as if debating whether to draw him into their planning. His face burning, Galan lurched to his feet. He imagined he could hear a few derisive chuckles as he followed the queen's exit route.

Giving in to his panic, he rushed through the halls seeking the safety of his chambers. If only he could relax the awful immobility of his face before it froze forever.

But when the door at last closed behind him, there was no chance to drop the mask. For inside his chambers waited a courtier of Auberlain, dressed in her green and gray. He wore a long-browed hat clamped low on his head, his face in shadows.

When the man looked up, Galan was stunned to see his Uncle William. His uncle's wild mane was smoothed with grease and tied tight at the neck. His beard was trimmed, his hands clean.

"I hope you don't mind," he said. "I convinced the boys to let me in. I didn't want to wait in the halls lest some old servant deduce me in my guise."

"How?" said Galan, in a near croak.

"A member of the delegation stopped by the roadhouse and I ... befriended him," said William. "It was the chance of a lifetime, to lose myself in the throng and see the court again."

William was staring at Galan with those uncanny eyes. Galan looked away, finding the two servant boys huddled on their mat. He focused on them as William talked. They were brothers, sons of Minnie in the kitchen. After all these days, he didn't know their names; odd that. The younger brother was much under the sway of the elder, it seemed to Galan.

"She was magnificent. Stood her ground like a soldier, dancing quarter-time around that stupid general. You could learn quite a bit from her."

Galan snapped his gaze back to William, who was strutting like a rooster in his stolen garb. Why was he here, what did he want?

What do they want? That was the game Rose had taught him to play whenever he was approached by some new person at court. You are the king's son, she'd said with a gloating smile. You have power. They want something from you. What do they want? Rose had elaborated all the ways this equation might play out: The servant who wants to do just enough work without getting a slap; the matron forcing her child on a young prince to curry favor with the queen; and so on. What do they want? That's all you need to know, said his grandmother Rose, about power.

What did William want? So long out in the woods, did he long to return to the privileged life of a royal? Did he think to be king himself?

"It is ill-done to see one of king's blood in the colors of our most untrustworthy neighbor."

William's face flushed angrily. Then the scowl erased itself, much as the servants did when caught off guard.

"Ah, my boy, don't confuse the man with his guise. Or the actor with the role. You and I, we understand what it is to wear a mask to hide our true selves. But I am not like you, I am not trapped by my birthright. I do as I please, Galan ... Think of it. ... Freedom from all this," said William, gesturing dismissively at the room, the royal emblem hanging over the hearth.

"You're no king, boy. Your mother was born to rule. Let her! Come away with me, let's leave this behind ... You and I, we're not trapped by the concerns that bind ordinary men. We have the power to do as we please. Only you must use it! ... I can show you a world you've never known, life outside your royal cage."

What was it Magritte had said? Beguiling like a snake. It seemed to Galan that his uncle was trying to speak to him again with his eyes, to whisper in his ear. He was back in the room above the roadhouse, submitting in the dark to his uncle's expert ministrations. Betraying Jonathan.

With a shudder of revulsion, he wrenched his gaze away from his uncle. He lurched to the chamber door. Behind him, he heard William laughing.

"Make your own rules, boy! That's real power!"

Galan staggered out into the hall, moving with the flow of people headed to the castle courtyard. He had to get out. His throat was tightening. In a moment he would have a seizure of the lungs, as from his childhood days. A little boy gasping for breath. And not finding it. He *must* get out.

As he passed the cloakroom, his uncle's ruse gave him an idea. Since the funeral, he'd twice tried to see Jonathan. Both times, the guards at the gate had stopped him and politely asked him to seek leave of the queen first.

Waiting until no one was about, he grabbed one of the Auberlain cloaks, pulling the hood far across his face. This was dangerous, donning the colors of the enemy. But he didn't matter, really. Who was he, anyway? The queen's strange son, the silent one. The odd bird, the weakling. The queer.

He waited until a crunch of people entered the courtyard, then blended in with them to walk free of the castle.

All that day, the sky had grown ever heavier with dense gray clouds. The long overdue snow was finally falling as Galan left the roadhouse. Jonathan had refused to let him take the Auberlain cloak, instead returning him his own plain one. Galan wrapped the familiar leather close about his face, breathing in the smell of sweat and skin. It seemed so long ago already, his idyll in the hills. He trudged through the dark streets.

The hours in Jonathan's room at the roadhouse had clarified something within Galan; although if asked, he could not have said what. Jonathan had wept with shame as he told Galan of his encounter with the strange-eyed man at the inn. Galan had comforted him, with kisses and more, but had not shared his own similar story. Why was he protecting his uncle, this villain who used a royal gift so basely?

He passed an open square where a group of men were drunkenly calling for vengeance against Auberlain. Even the common folk weren't fooled by this tale of robbers attacking the royal camp. Where was his own anger for the murders of his father and brother? Why did he need Jonathan to tell him what his duty was, or his mother, or some drunken louts shouting in the snow?

The guards let him pass with no interruption. Like a man entranced, Galan went to his room and fetched his father's ring. He made his way to the tallest of the three towers, climbing the spiral stairs to the open turret.

As the snow fell, the young prince dropped to his knees and prayed to his father for guidance – as one king to another. Deep in his prayers he didn't hear the door to the tower roof open.

"My lord picks a strange place for his bedtime prayers."

Hearing René's voice, Galan slid the ring onto the long finger of his left hand, signet side hidden in his fist. He got off his knees and turned to face René, who had strolled over to the low brick wall that ringed the lookout. He leaned against the bricks, looking out at the eagle-eye view of Hyperia Court.

"Is it not pretty, my lord? The first snow of winter."

Galan came to stand by René. He looked out at the many lighted windows, the columns of smoke streaming up, each like a sentry standing guard atop its roof. The snow clouds hung heavy and low, smothering the sky with their spillage.

"You will never rule this kingdom," said Galan.

A mocking smile devoured René's face.

"Strong words, my lord! Where were they when your mother needed them, a hapless woman defending the crown?"

"You will never rule here."

René continued with his quips, and a roaring came back into Galan's ears. In spite of himself, he couldn't stop noticing how devilishly handsome was René.

"... but there is no reason our two families cannot be united. Perhaps my lord would consent to marry his poor brother's widow. ... No, I don't suppose he would. Well there is your mother. Were she a bit younger I might yet take her for a wife. What a rogering that would be! But alas, too many sands of the hourglass have fallen to trust in that womb."

The shock of such impertinence froze Galan.

"Of course, there is the other matter of her ... temperament. She knows not the ways of a true lady of the court, who would never stride about like a man. But then she were ever a country lass, no? She and that crone of a mother ..."

René turned to face Galan, switching from taunts to the overt coquetry he had used to seduce Galan those years ago.

"'Tis a pity my lord himself can bear no child. He is of meek disposition and would make a comely lass. Such lips, so hard to resist. I remember their sweetness."

He moved closer, as if to kiss Galan. He reached down and touched himself, his hand cupping and fondling the pouch of his breeches.

"Shall my lord show us what a clever lassie he can be?"

A red cloud passed in front of Galan's eyes. The red of rubies, the red eye of the lion. In a swirling red vision, Galan saw René pressing something into Catherine's hand; and then Catherine nervously opening a drawer on Magritte's dressing table. What Galan had known all along suddenly broke through the surface: René had killed his father and brother, brothers. If not by his own hand, by conspiracy.

When the scarlet veil lifted, he found himself strangling René. His ring hand pressed the signet deep into the side of René's throat.

René struggled and tossed, and the two men fell to the ground. But Galan retained the upper hand, squeezing with all his might as René's face swelled and grew purple. The desperate hands clawing at Galan's grip grew weaker and finally fell away.

Galan was still throttling René, he didn't know for how long, when a hand fell on his shoulder.

It was the sergeant of the guard, Conor; and behind him, two others.

Conor helped him to his feet, giving a brief glance to René's still form.

"Well done, my lord. The lion's cub roars at last!"

Words failed Galan. Conor barked an order to the two guards, who turned and raced down the stairs.

It seemed to Galan that time was moving very slowly. He watched as the guards returned with a blanket, a length of rope and two potato sacks weighted with stones. The snow was already starting to cover René's inert form.

"My lord should return to his chamber," said

131

Conor. "We will attend to matters here."

The guards had stripped away René's shoes and embroidered suit and were binding the sacks to his body.

"What will you do?"

Conor gave a harsh laugh.

"Why, we'll toss him out with all the other turds!"

He pointed to the far side of the turret, which capped a long windowless wall down to the sewage pond behind the castle.

"My lord bided his time well," said Conor approvingly. "The pond will be frozen by morning."

Conor looked down and nudged René's body with his boot.

"He won't be so pretty in the spring."

One of the guards exclaimed, pointing to René's neck where the figure of a lion had been branded in scarlet, etched cleanly down to the curve of its narrow tail.

The men stared. Then as one, the three dropped to one knee and bowed their heads.

"We swear our fealty to the new king," said Conor.

"Long live the king," answered the guards.

Galan watched as the men silently lowered the body on a loop of rope. A few feet above the water, they heaved and pulled to create a gentle swing. At the right moment, Conor released his end of the rope and the heavily-laden sack spooled off into the deepest water. Or rather, onto the ice, which had already formed atop the pond. For a long moment it seemed the evidence of their crime might stay exposed in full view. But then the surface splintered and René vanished into his new kingdom.

One of guards quickly pulled the rope back up the side of the castle wall and wound it around his elbow and thumb. Rene's clothes were gone. It was as if nothing had happened.

"Now go," said Conor.

Galan turned, and then stopped.

"Conor. My liegeman, you know him well, is housed at a roadhouse. The Two Stags."

He took off his father's ring and handed it to the sergeant.

"I bid you show him this ring and bring him to my chamber."

Struggling for just an instant, the sergeant dropped his head.

"Aye, my lord."

When the bells began tolling at dawn, Galan imagined that his night's work had been discovered. A royal nephew of Auberlain has been murdered. He would be imprisoned. There would be a trial, perhaps a war. He had played into their hands and removed himself from the game.

But it was strange, the bells tolling for a foreign visitor. Such a clamor was for royalty — weddings, births, deaths.

His mother was dead. He knew it without any doubt.

Galan dressed and headed to her chambers. He passed through a growing throng of alarmed courtiers and servants. Elise opened the door and let him in.

Magritte was lying in bed, the bedclothes pulled up under her arms. Her bony white cat sat at the foot of the bed, watching Galan with rheumy blue eyes. Elise had attempted to pull Magritte's hair back and smooth out the bedclothes. But Galan had the impression his mother had died a most violent death. There was blood incrusted in the broken fingernails of her hands, which were now clasped below her bosom. An animal savageness lingered about her face.

Elise handed him the letter, and then retired to her alcove. Galan slumped down on to the bench where he had dined with her so many times. As in everything else befitting a noble lady, his mother had worked hard at learning the graces of reading and writing. As he read her words he could hear her voice speaking them.

My dear son and King,

As you read this, know that I am dead. And so, too, Auberlain's claim on our throne. When the jackbird lays her eggs in the wren's nest, the wren must pluck out the imposters lest they kill her own chicks. It is a foul deed done by my mother's darkest arts, and there is no recovery for me. I die by my own hand, a life for a life.

Still my soul is blighted until you give back that which I took. Go to her, Galan. Separate her from that treacherous brother. Marry her. Give her the life that I have taken, give Hyperia the son it needs. There can be no peace between our countries while Hyperia has no heir.

Do not let René take Catherine from the castle. It must be proved that she carries no child. If she leaves our walls, all is lost. For any babe may be put in its stead.

A king can be many men, Galan. But he must be a father. Let not your own strange tastes detour you from your destiny. I thought to tell you once, of her vision ... She saw it. Standing over your cradle, Galan. You would be king. Not Jacques. Not Phillip, who died yesterday and is hidden in the great oak chest.

I can see things as they are ... but my mother, Galan. My mother could see things that will be. Might be, could be. She saw her daughter married to a king, and it came to pass.

She saw you, Galan, sitting on the throne in a time of peace and prosperity such as Hyperia has never seen.

I pray you make it so.

The letter went on to describe how he must have her rose quartz burned with her and Phillip's bodies, and then retrieve it from the pyre ashes. His mother's careful letters were taking on a scratchy look, as if the queen were struggling to hold the quill.

In fire will it be cleansed. My humble stone bears no power save one, to calm and clear the thoughts. The true power lies within you, as it does in all of us.

I bid you be steadfast in your rule.

Think kindly of your Queen and mother

Magritte

Below her name, written in lighter ink as if something she wanted to share outside her formal correspondence, she had scrawled:

I fear the poison's touch

Magritte's final words, her one show of weakness, split Galan's heart. As the white cat looked on, he dropped his head and arms onto the table and cried.

Two Auberlain sentries were posted outside Catherine's door. But the Hyperian guards accompanying Galan obliged his entry into her chambers. He ignored the protests of her ladies in waiting and came to her bedside.

Catherine rested much as Magritte had, hands clasped below her bosom. Except the sheets rose and fell softly with her breath. There were dark circles under her eyes, and a smell of woman's blood at the bedside. Blood under her fingernails, too.

"How goes it, lady?"

She seemed little surprised to see him. When she spoke her words were breathy, as if it pained her to speak.

"The bells toll my loss. Such a clamor for one tiny life, such a little speck of flesh."

"The bells sound for the queen, who even now lies cold upon her bower. I have just come from there."

Catherine received the news silently. She seemed to be having an inner conversation with herself that gradually leaked out into spoken words.

"Shall I show the young prince? No, that would not be ladylike. Besides, he has no interest in a woman's rose. Shall I tell him? Shall I speak it? She came to me, young prince. Clawing and scratching. A white cat with queen's eyes. Hungry for the mouse."

With a feeble thrust, she pushed down the

bedclothes. Her robe was pulled all the way up to her breasts; her naked loins rested on a clean white cloth, in a circle of blood.

As the ladies rushed to pull the blanket back up, she pointed at the many scratches on her abdomen and inner thighs, surrounding on all sides the hairy mound of her womanhood. Scratches as if some beast had attacked her in her most vulnerable place.

Galan thought of his mother's fingernails and shuddered.

"I know," he said. "I'm sorry."

The ladies tried to force Galan from her bedside, shushing and clucking. It was a formidable assault, but he held tight to the bedpost.

"Where is my brother," cried Catherine, feverishly.

"Your brother has gone away," said Galan. "He has been called away." He held her eye with clear meaning until she turned away. She gave an indifferent little shrug.

We all overlook her, thought Galan. We barely notice her. She is the vessel. Yet she was a pretty thing, in her quiet way. Her skin was clear and she had good teeth. Even in her lowest hour, she retained a simple dignity.

Galan found himself thinking about Catherine; really, for the first time. She was 17 when she married Jacques. So now she would be 22, 23 years old. Not young anymore; but she had proved herself capable of conception. This sad bed was no fault of hers.

What had been her life? Raised in a court, with all the people watching; all her life. Never a private moment. Traded to a foreign kingdom as if she were a prized brood mare. And then life with Jacques, who was a brute. And Magritte for a kinswoman, there's a tyrant. And then her own brother. Did he force himself upon her? Or bring some stranger to her?

He found himself feeling sorry for this wrung-out little wren. Of all the people at court, this one best understood what Galan's own life had been.

"We're all alone," he said. "It's just us two."

"Don't send me away," she whispered. "Don't send me back."

He sat with Catherine until she nodded off. He warned his guards to be alert to any attempts to remove the ailing lady from her chamber.

Galan kept his mother's rose quartz. It was not burned as she had directed. For many years, King Galan consulted the stone in the manner of his mother. Holding the quartz gently in his fingertips, his head cocked to one side as she had. Regarding the glassy sides of the quartz and the cloudy pinkness within.

But as any mage can tell you, in a time of chaos, visions in a magic crystal shift like blowing leaves. Sometimes Galan saw a life for himself of self-sacrifice and duty to his kingdom, a life that still held a small corner in it for private happiness with Jonathan. But in the early years of his reign, the view was less rosy; more often a dimly-lit path of drastic measures to secure the safety of Hyperia. With the abyss looming one false step away.

What was a vision, anyway, but a wish or fear painted in one's mind to row towards or away from? What had been his grandmother's gift, her arrogance to select one landscape above all the others in the deck?

In time, Galan gave up seeking an oracle in the stone. He used it as the queen had advised, to clear his thoughts on this or that problem of state. It was then he was glad the stone had not been purged, for he sought his mother's canniness. Gazing into the milky pinkness, asking: What would Magritte do? Sometimes he heeded her counsel. In this way Queen Magritte lived on past her death in her son's heart and innermost reflections. Her wisdom infused his decisions; he honored her boldness in his actions.

Could any parent ask for more?

As he learned the ways of statecraft, King Galan better understood King Arnow. Catherine helped him see things in a kinder light, talking of her own father and her impressions of Arnow from her years at court as Jacques' wife. Knowing the tale of rapacious William, Galan could see how his father acted decisively to clear the court anew of a family blight. Of course it could be argued that Arnow should have known the essential differences in character between his brother and son. But Arnow had been preparing the way for Jacques, wanting no unseemly distractions from the third son. That's just the way it was.

In time, Galan came to see some of his estrangement from his parents had been of his own making. When he had first realized his own strangeness, he had sought to hide it, and himself, from discovery. Closing a door to those closest to him, rejecting them before they could reject him.

Grudges and disappointments fell away and finer feelings endured.

Fear, also, was conquered; or rather, controlled, as much as any man may. Although never completely free of his surges of panic, Galan hardened himself to weather the moments of terror. He learned to not fear the possibility of fear. It would come, it would pass. Like many troubles. Thoughts and fears were like leaves upon a stream, floating; tumbling over the rocks, disappearing downstream. And he would remain.

The rogue prince William dropped out of sight. Galan had resolved to show kindness neither of them had known, and restore his uncle to court. But perhaps William had known he would not be able to practice his avaricious arts under his nephew's eye.

One day the rose quartz was misplaced by a servant. King Galan grieved the loss of his keepsake. But his mother was not lost. By then he knew all the people who had loved him and been loved by him lived on inside him. If one was lucky, it was a crowded chamber: Spirits jostling about, bumping elbows to warm their hands at the hearth.

This conviction, along with its companion – the quiet belief that he, too, would be cherished in the hearts of a few – illuminated the life of Galan, the man. Important, in its way, as the many good acts of his kingship.

Where, then, to end the tale of the prodigal prince who became king? Does the rose quartz show an old man on his deathbed, surrounded by his children and grandchildren, his dearest friend with his own family? A dying old man thinking what they all do: So soon, so fast!

Or is the young king-to-be walking slowly down the hall to his room, after a long day of meetings with his advisors? The funerals tomorrow, his coronation the next, and the expulsion of the Auberlain delegation the day after.

Does Galan pause at his door, hearing boyish laughter? Does he pull it open a crack to watch Jonathan sitting on the floor teaching a game of sticks to the two chamber boys. Stacking the twigs in a precarious tower soon tumbled, like all plans of man. A smile from beautiful Jonathan and its weary answer from Galan.

Is that the place to leave off? Should we try the stone anew? Throw the cards?

Only Grandmother Rose knows. And she's not saying.

About the author

David M. Hancock is a longtime journalist and fiction writer living in New York City. For the last decade, he has been a web editor at CBS News. Prior to that, he held various gigs in the New York tech boom of the late 1990s. Before coming to New York, he worked 10 years as a reporter at *The Miami Herald*, where he shared in a staff-wide Pulitizer Prize for coverage of Hurricane Andrew. He won various other honors in Texas as a Mexico reporter for *The El Paso Times* and *The Brownsville Herald*.

His debut novel "Tricks Gone Bad" is available on Amazon.com.

For more about his work and upcoming projects, check the author's page on Amazon.com or visit www.AbysmalAntics.com. Write him at davidmhancock@abysmalantics.com.

Also from David M Hancock on Amazon.com: "Tricks Gone Bad"

In the high desert west of Ciudad Juarez, Mexico, a passionate interlude between two men goes off the tracks. A young journalist for The El Paso Times reports the crime but misses the key questions. Why would a man with a successful career, a home and loving family, risk everything for a casual encounter with a stranger? And why did he have to die?

After covering the Juarez murder, the young journalist is soon embroiled in his own trick gone bad; a betrayal which could cast a permanent shadow over his life. And it's not the only time the reporter risks personal and professional ruin without asking important questions.

In five interlocking scenes that span 15 years and four cities, author David M. Hancock points a searing white light at a life of gay cruising and deadline reporting. It's all about adrenalin in these vignettes, whether the reporter is covering a young woman's murder in Coral Gables or making a 3 a.m. drug run with a Miami Beach go-go boy. Or debating whether to stab a shady character in New York City.

"Tricks Gone Bad" – An erotic tapestry of fact and fiction that begins and ends with a real-life murder in the Chihuahua desert. Cunningly-told moments moored in the misty suspension of consequences required for sex with strangers.

Tricks Gone Bad

CIUDAD JUAREZ, 1985 – Back before the Internet siphoned off the mystery of human intercourse, men of a certain ilk had secret gathering places. Every city, town or two-horse hamlet had a place or two of convergence for men with an itch to scratch. Each acting to his nature: Peacocks preening in the moonlight, coyotes lurking in the shadows. The setting might be a park or rest stop subtly enhanced by hovering spirits; a forest or isolated beach consecrated by lust. Maybe you got directions from runes scratched on a bathroom stall. Or some kneeling acolyte told you as you buttoned your jeans. Perhaps you stumbled upon it in your own restless rambles: An unremarkable locale unmasked by the telltale glimmer of fairy dust. The druid in you could smell the billowing sexual energy of a sacred grove. And when you returned later and saw the hungry animals prowling, beasts like yourself, you thought with satisfaction: Aha! I knew it!

Not all hijinks happen in the midnight hour, of course; or off the beaten trail. Male sexual energy is so irrepressible that it bubbles up right under the noses of unsuspecting citizens going about their daily rounds.

Libraries, in particular, are prone to attract adventurers with other than literary pursuits. Double agents posing with a prop book or magazine, watching the herd with wolf eyes.

It's torn down now in the name of urban revitalization. But the old public library in El Paso, Texas, was a known venue – doubling as a source of

144

archived knowledge and sexual connection.

The library was a modest building of no great account, built onto one side of a nondescript park in downtown El Paso.

A shabby building, really. But if its stacks could talk – what a tale it would be of covert glances, hands accidentally brushing against asses, bathroom quickies and assignations taken off-site.

David is already intimately familiar with that particular library when its dual nature comes up in a tragic and scandalous news story he is reporting.

David is on the phone right now speaking with the Chihuahua state judicial police chief. It's a little past 7 p.m. and David is sitting at his desk in the fluorescent-lit brightness of The El Paso Times newsroom. He has just returned from his daily trek to Ciudad Juarez – an hour sitting in traffic on the international bridge.

David's back is to the windows of the newsroom, where the sun is descending in a burst of blinding orange that will wind its way through a series of vivid reds and profound purples. Another glorious Southwest sunset, the kind that visitors stop and gape at; but one that barely registers with locals.

All around him, the newsroom bustles with the organized chaos of a newspaper preparing to go to print.

At 26, David's journalism career has brought him to the far western tip of Texas, where El Paso and Ciudad Juarez share a parched, concrete-lined river bed that was once the mighty Rio Grande.

El Paso and Ciudad Juarez: A provincial West Texas city joined at the hip with an unfettered Mexican metropolis three times its size. David envisions the unequal relationship like two girls meeting at a flower mart on the riverside. A prim young woman from a West Texas pioneer family selecting floral arrangements; and a dark-haired cantina girl looking for a man who owes her money. They nod at each other and move on with their different lives.

David speaks Spanish and covers Juarez for *The El Paso Times.* He's intrepid and produces a lot of copy, which is key for small newspapers. He looks at the Juarez papers every morning for something good to pick up; or works on his own stuff. David was a foreign exchange student in high school and brings that respectful, multi-cultural vibe to the job. When he speaks Spanish he has a looser, more expansive personal style. Subtleties and ambiguities fall by the wayside. David is blond and good looking; a Juarez journalist once told him they call him "Superman" behind his back.

It's a typically bad phone connection and David is having to shout his questions in Spanish. These high-volume interrogations used to amuse the copy desk, the paper's blessed regiment of off-center wackadoodles. But now they just roll their eyes at each other and sigh.

The chief is giving David the latest on a missing El Paso man. There's just enough time for him to get something in the 8 p.m. state edition run. It's a good scoop that will rankle his competitor at The El Paso Herald-Post, a tiny afternoon daily that won't go to press until noon the next day. The El Paso police department will also be annoyed that David is getting the story from the Mexicans before they can sanitize the information.

Fuck 'em all!

The Chihuahua police chief is a loathsome man; David is sure he is corrupt. The chief takes unusual pleasure in delivering the details, based on statements from a young Mexican vagrant they arrested that afternoon. David wonders how they got such a thorough confession in such a short amount of time. But that's a story for another day.

The victim is an American businessman man who has been missing for several days. According to the suspect's story, the American man picked him up at the downtown El Paso library. They drove in the man's van out to an isolated spot west of Ciudad Juarez where they drank beer and smoked weed.

The police chief seems a little drunk or hopped up. He takes sensual relish in describing how the suspect told police the American man sucked his dick and then allowed himself to be anally fucked. Is this some Mexican imperialism at play? Slipping the Mexican *verga* to Uncle Sam? Or is he trying to make a point to a U.S. journalist that this man brought it upon himself, and that Mexico is not to blame?

The party in the desert goes downhill. The El Paso man is stabbed several times, run over with his own van and left dead or dying. The young Mexican was picked up that afternoon driving the man's van. He was later persuaded to lead police to the remote area where the El Paso man's body was decomposing.

After he hangs up, David turns to the copy desk and recounts in a theatrical way the sordid tale. He raises the question of whether they should withhold the salacious details of the hookup. But he quickly quashes that in the name of "the story." David pretends to be sad about how this news will hurt the man's family; but it is all theater.

At this point in his journalism career – and for many years after – David is in ambulance-driver mode. He chronicles a lot of dirt and death in a respectful manner. But it doesn't reach him inside. It's not until his 40s – when he's grappled firsthand with the finality of death – when his Iron Man suit begins to crack on the really sad stories.

David bangs out a story for the West Texas-New Mexico run, making deadline as always. He then has two hours to refine his story for the city edition. He decides to call up the victim's family and stick this needle in their collective eye.

"My dad is not a queer," shouts the dead man's son, a college kid with tears in his voice. David does the sympathetic, sorry-to-disturb-you bit and gets a few quotes for the local edition.

He does a follow-up story the next day, including another call to the family. He listens patiently to abuse about his front page story and then harvests more quotes from the overwhelmed son. With no new details on the crime, David makes his story more laudatory of the victim, a family man who was a mid-level executive at one of the many U.S. twin plants that operate in Juarez. That would explain the man's willingness to cross the border with his new acquaintance, thinks David; but he doesn't belabor the point.

There is a value in telling these stories, David tells himself. These things do happen. People need to know. It's a rationale that serves him through the years as he regularly latches onto people during the worst moments of their lives.

The grief is there, he thinks. Whether reporters stir the pot or not. The grief is not going away. David keeps his eye on the big picture –

getting the story for the greater good. He doesn't beat himself up over the methodology.

Two front page articles; then David is down and done with his cautionary tale about sex and death in the desert. David rolls on to the next story.

Is it really just a few weeks later, though, that David finds himself playing peekaboo in the stacks of that same downtown El Paso library?

It's not that David is insensible to the risks of casual sex. He gets it: Lowlifes prey on gays, confident that they won't report abuses to the police. That "vagrant" in the desert; that wasn't his first day at the rodeo. He didn't make the leap from first sexual encounter with a man to murdering a john in one fell swoop. He would have a psychic history of larceny and exploitation, if not an actual paper trail.

It wasn't the victim's first dance, either.

David gets it. He just doesn't care.